Pr
The Hitchh

"Alden weaves lived-in details about life on the ocean with a rich cast of characters that will whisk you away on a vacation without leaving your living room."

—Sara Whitney, author of the *Tempt Me* series

"*The Hitchhiker in Panama* is a delicious cocktail of sailing, wanderlust, exotic destinations, and steamy romance. Be warned: Once you step aboard, you may never want to leave!"

—Trish Doller, author of *Float Plan*

Have you read the prequel short story,
The Night in Lover's Bay?

See how Marcella met the crew of Eik and started on her adventure. It's available to subscribers of my newsletter for free. Sign up and get your copy at lizalden.com.

Also by Liz Alden:

The Hitchhiker in Panama

A Love and Wanderlust Novel

Liz Alden

THE HITCHHIKER IN PANAMA

Copyright © 2021 Liz Alden

All rights reserved.

ISBN-13: 978-1-954705-02-9

Library of Congress Control Number: 2021904970

Published by Liz Alden, First Edition

Cover Design by E Stokes Creative

Developmental Editor: Tiffany Tyer

Copy Editor: Kaitlin Severini

Proofreader: David G Brown, Darling Axe Editing

To my husband.
There is no one else I could have circumnavigated the globe with. Twenty-five days at sea? We make it look easy.

To everyone who said I should write a book: this is not what you had in mind. Thank you for encouraging me anyway.

One

My cabdriver was trying to abandon me in the jungles of Panama.

Or at least that was what I thought when I woke up.

"Señorita, estamos aquí."

I lifted my head and blinked lazily out the rear passenger-side window. When the view didn't make sense, I blinked harder and rubbed my eyes, trying to forestall panic.

There was nothing but jungle. I'd been traveling for nearly forty hours: three flights beginning in my native Sydney, a nap in a hostel, a train, and now my taxi was trying to dump me in the middle of the Panamanian jungle.

"Oh no," I murmured.

"Señorita." My driver pointed out the other side of the car.

There was my hotel, a small concrete building with a sign that read "Hotel & Marina." I grinned sheepishly at him through the rearview mirror and mumbled "Gracias" as I opened the door and climbed out. He waited while I grabbed both of my backpacks from the trunk, and as soon as I shut the door, he was bumping down the gravel road again.

I stared up at the building, my stomach a jumble of emotions. Planning this trip had seemed so easy: with a click or a scroll of my mouse, I could be in Buenos Aires, Svalbard, or Thailand. Now, with the actual adventure staring me in the face, I was terrified.

Hola. Me llamo Lila Ryan. Tengo reserva de hotel.

Tengo reserva de hotel.

I took a deep breath and pushed the door open. A middle-aged woman sat at the front desk and smiled as I approached and dropped my backpacks down at my feet.

"Hola," I warbled. *"Me llamo Lila Ryan. Tengo . . . tengo res . . ."* I blew out a breath of frustration and my cheeks heated.

"Hola, Lila. My name is Paula." Her English was perfect, with a beautiful accent. My tension faded away and I grinned.

2

"Hi. Sorry." I put my hands to my burning cheeks. "My cabdriver didn't speak any English, and my Spanish is obviously terrible."

"That is okay. The yachties are mostly English-speakers, so I get a lot of practice."

While Paula checked me in, we chatted about the marina amenities and my upcoming adventure. The knowledge that I was in the right place and had a bed to sleep in tonight took the pressure off, and with the adrenaline of travel winding down, I was getting sleepy.

"Here." Paula handed me my room key. "I have upgraded you to marina view instead of jungle view. For inspiration."

She directed me to the stairs and I climbed, half-heartedly dragging my stuff behind me. I opened the door to my small room and dumped my backpacks on the bed.

The room was expensive, more than I'd budgeted for, but here in the marina there was only one option, and I had to be in the marina.

I poked around the room until I got to the window. Finally I saw what I'd come here for. Below my second-story window, the marina docks extended out into the water and the masts of hundreds of sailboats rose like trees in a forest. The stress of travel, the worries over missed flights and overslept alarms, the words of my mother telling me that taking three months to travel alone on a budget would never work . . . it all washed away.

One of these boats would take me on the first leg of my adventure: through the Panama Canal.

———————

IT WAS FIVE IN THE MORNING AND STILL BLACK outside, but thanks to too much napping, my body was replenished and ready for the day to begin. I dressed, ate a muesli bar, and slipped out of my room, mindful of possible neighbors, and exited the hotel through the back.

I inhaled deeply, breathing in the scents of Panama: the humidity, the salt air, and a refreshing vegetation smell. The marina and hotel were far enough away from the dirty, smoggy city of Colón to avoid the stench, and I could breathe deeply out here.

Paula had assured me the area here was safe and that there were twenty-four-hour security guards, even though the marina was remote. I turned left and walked along the water's edge on the dock, enjoying the morning stillness. After half an hour of wandering the shore, the darkness began to change. Twilight drew a silhouette on my left, the jungle still steeped in shadows, but the sky was lightening above it.

I avoided walking in the trees, and instead I found an area where sailboats of every shape and size were stored on dry land. It was surreal to see the undersides of the boats, like viewing an iceberg beneath the waterline. The air was deathly still and quiet, as if I'd wandered into a graveyard of steel and fiberglass.

Eventually I made my way back to the docks. The sun glinted over the tops of the masts and all around me people were beginning their day, climbing down from their boats or opening hatches, doing all sorts of boat-life things.

Most of the sailors were older than I was—spry pensioners who gave me a parade of smiles and polite hellos as I walked up and down the docks. I meandered, wondering about each boat and its story.

There were small sailboats with cluttered decks and shiny wood, and luxurious catamarans that made me think of the pictures my best friend Dani had taken on her trip to Greece when we were sixteen—a trip my mother had forbidden me to go on.

Someone caught my eye up ahead, a young man walking down the dock, coming all the way from the end.

5

I tried to focus on the sailboats, but I kept glancing at him, and the closer he got, the more I liked what I saw. He was broad and fair-skinned, dressed casually in a T-shirt and shorts that showed more thigh than not—very European fashion.

When he was just a few boats away, our eyes met. His lips grew into a sly grin, and my heart skipped a beat. I looked away, but just before we passed, my eyes caught his again.

"*God morgen.*" His voice was low, accented, and even though I knew it was a simple greeting, I blushed and forced myself not to glance back. Definitely European.

Ah, what a wonderful distraction to my morning.

I kept walking, hoping to see the guy again on my way back to the shore, but he didn't return. On the next pier, I was startled by a noise up ahead of me. It began deep and guttural, resonating through the jungle and crescendoing to a roar. The kind of sound that made humans know they were prey.

I froze, listening intently, though no one else seemed to be concerned.

"Howler monkeys," came a voice to my right. A balding man with glasses and a goatee was sitting in his boat with a tablet and a mug of coffee.

"Seriously?" I was stunned. "They sound like dinosaurs." The howls continued, the monkeys answering one another from tree to tree. "Should I be worried?"

He grinned at me. "Nah, they don't come out of the jungle—you're just fine. But if you'd like a cup of coffee . . . ?" He gestured with his mug.

I bit my lip, torn between the prospect of sheltering from a hypothetical monkey attack and the safety factor of climbing into a boat with a random man. Just as I was about to make an excuse, a woman's head poked up from inside the boat.

"Hello there, dear." She gingerly held a pot of steaming coffee while she climbed out of the boat. "Peter's offering some caffeine, eh?" She winked at me while refilling her partner's mug.

"Yes, I'd love some."

The woman gestured me over and showed me how to climb onto the boat. Her white pixie-cut hair, weathered skin, and heavy laugh lines around her eyes pointed to a happy life out of doors. She smiled so much, she had tan lines in her laugh lines.

"Welcome to *Silver Lining*. This is Peter, I'm Edith, and here's your mug."

"Thanks. I'm Lila."

"Lila," Edith repeated, settling down onto a cushioned bench. "Lila with an accent. Are you an Aussie?"

"I am, good ear. Are you . . . ?" I hedged, unsure whether they were Canadian or American.

"Canadians," Edith confirmed. "But this boat's been our home for, oh, eight years now?"

Peter, who had returned his attention to his tablet, nodded.

"Where's your boat?" Edith asked.

"I don't have one, actually. I read online about how boats going through the canal sometimes need extra crew members, and that if I came here, I might find a ride."

"Oof, I hope you aren't in a rush. The season hasn't quite picked up around here yet. It's still early. How much time do you have?"

"I'm pretty flexible," I said. "After the canal I'll be making my way south, backpacking for a while."

"How fun. Back in my day, we didn't do that, what do you call it? A gap year?"

"A gap year," Peter agreed.

"You know," Edith said, "parents' house, college, marriage."

I smiled into my mug. "Did you always know you were going to go on a sailing adventure together?"

"Not at all. My kids were appalled when I told them I was taking off with my new husband"—she gestured to Peter— "to go sailing. But when the kids are grown, what's to stop us? It'll be grandkids soon, and then our health will deteriorate. Best to go now."

Peter interrupted us. "How long have you been backpacking?"

"This is my first stop, so I'm just getting started."

"How exciting. How did you choose here?"

"I had just graduated uni, and I was excited for life to start—you know, a good career, marriage, kids—but also . . . I've never been anywhere. And it's been pointed out that my viewpoint may be a little"—I chewed on my lip while trying to think of a nicer term— "narrow-minded."

"Your parents?" Edith guessed.

"Yeah, nah. My parents aren't big travelers either. They've never done anything like this, which is part of the appeal. I wanted to get away, but I only had a few months to work and earn some money. I have a limited budget, so I chose Latin America."

As we sipped our coffees, I asked Peter and Edith a million questions about their boat and their travels.

They told me stories beyond my wildest dreams, of native tribes in the islands and mega-yacht neighbors, until we were interrupted by a crackling sound downstairs.

Edith jumped up. "Time for the net. Why don't we listen in and then you can join us for breakfast, Lila?"

I had read about the VHF net on a blog post while I was planning my trip. Every morning boaters swapped check-ins, reports, and announcements over the radio, including social activities, field trips, and buy-sell-trade offers. It was similar to listening to the morning news on your local radio station but interactive. I was depending on it to be my key to finding a boat that needed a crew member.

"Oh, I was going to listen in at the office. Paula said I could announce that I was available to crew."

"Just do it here. No need to fuss." Edith waved her hand and led me downstairs. The interior of *Silver Lining* was small and dark; I had to let my eyes adjust to get my bearings. The only light filtered in from the doorway I'd just come down, but Edith quickly moved to open the curtains above our heads.

I pivoted around and took their boat in, the small kitchen on the left, a dining booth to my right, all the things that made it a home: a swinging basket of oranges, apples, and cucumbers; a laptop in a thick case as if prepared to survive a nuclear war; a wall hanging, a maze of black-and-red fabric with visible stitches around the edges forming the shape of an animal with a tail—maybe a monkey?

Edith pointed out a radio with a variety of dials and showed me how to press the button to talk. We then listened to the net together, with Edith taking notes: dominoes today at four, a bus to the shopping mall on Tuesdays, swap meet Friday.

Finally the controller got to my part. "Next up, is there anyone listening who is in need of additional crew members to go through the canal, or anyone wanting to join a boat?"

I pressed the button, my fingers shaking. "Lila."

"Go ahead, Lila."

"Hello. My name is Lila. I arrived yesterday and I am staying at the hotel. I am looking to crew through the Panama Canal as soon as possible."

"Excellent, thank you, Lila," they responded. "Anyone else?" There were a few moments of silence. I crossed my fingers and closed my eyes, hoping that someone would chime in about needing crew and I would be lucky enough to get a lead on my first day. "Nothing heard. Lila, there are boats coming and going every day, and it's just starting to get busy here. Good luck, and we'll check in with you tomorrow. Moving on . . ."

I blew out a breath and slumped back, opening my eyes again. Edith patted my shoulder. "Buck up, you'll do it all again tomorrow."

Realistically, I had known that it was unlikely my first day would be successful, but my optimistic nature had taken a hit.

Edith and I refilled our coffees and went back up into the cockpit of the boat, where it was much cooler. Peter stayed down below to prepare brekkie.

"While our boat was hauled out," Edith said, "we didn't stay on it. Sometimes we had to stay in the marina's hotel. It's nice and cheap, but it's not a home, and every cent of money saved counts. But most of the time we relied on the kindness of our friends and slept in their boats. Why don't you let us return the boat karma, and come stay with us?"

I didn't know what to say. People invited total strangers to live with them? I thought about the cramped quarters downstairs and my light airy room in the hotel. Then I thought about my bank balance and carefully detailed budget.

"Think about it," Edith said. "Why don't I walk you through the marina this evening around happy hour and introduce you to a few people who may be looking for crew?"

Two

EDITH'S OFFER TO WALK ME AROUND THE DOCKS IN THE evening was invaluable. The sailors were out in the cooler temperatures, finishing their projects or cracking open a cold beer. We walked from boat to boat, and Edith knew everyone—not unsurprising, since *Silver Lining* had been in the marina for nearly a year. A handful of boats were looking for an additional crew member, but none of them fit my timetable.

As it was getting dark, and my stomach grumbled in hunger, Edith and I agreed to head back to *Silver Lining*. There was always tomorrow.

When we returned, Edith and I had our own sundowners—boat-speak for happy hour—in the cockpit while Peter cooked in the galley.

"You'd really be okay with me moving in?" I asked. "Even if it's a week or longer?"

Edith patted my hand. "I am absolutely sure."

"Did you talk to Peter about it?"

"PETE!" Edith shouted. "LILA IS GOING TO STAY WITH US!"

"Yes, dear," came his voice from down below. And that was that.

THE NEXT MORNING, I MOVED IN, CHECKING OUT OF the hotel with a very understanding Paula. When I showed up at *Silver Lining* with my bags, Edith led me downstairs and Peter set the coffeepot to brew.

She pointed to the back of the boat. "This is our cabin. The head—that's the bathroom—is through here." She waved to an open door. "Galley here on the port side, Peter's desk and a seating area on the starboard side. You'll be up here."

I stood awkwardly for a few moments while she bustled around, moving things out of the way.

Through the doorway was a small bedroom. Wedged up into the bow of the boat, the bed had a V-shaped cushion with a gap at the wide end. A tiny amount of floor space at this side of the bed contained bins and piles of unidentifiable boat things.

"It's not much; we usually use this room for storage. But it's free, so it's better than staying in the hotel, and you won't be spending much time in the room itself. This is a head in here"— Edith put her hand on a closed door just outside my new room— "but it's full of stuff, and being in a marina anyway, we use the bathrooms in the marina facilities. You can use the kitchen sink to brush your teeth on board. Everything else, go ashore."

I put my backpacks on the bed, as there was no other place to put them down in the room. When I pressed on the mattress, I found it stiff and unyielding. Was this a better option than the hotel room? *Free, free, free,* I reminded myself.

"Thank you so much for letting me stay here."

"You are welcome, dear. Now, make yourself at home, and don't let us old farts slow you down!"

AFTER I DUMPED MY MEAGER THINGS IN MY NEW ROOM, Peter and I drank coffee in the cockpit until the net. I got no leads on a position for the canal.

After breakfast, Edith rushed off to join the shuttle to the supermarket, which left me alone on the boat with Peter.

"What are your plans for the day?" he asked me.

I shrugged. "No plans. You?"

"Oh, I've got a pump I need to rebuild down in the bilge. It shouldn't take too long, though. I don't suppose you would want to help?"

I hesitated for a moment. It sounded like something completely outside of my expertise. But Peter and Edith were giving me a free place to stay; the least I could do was help out. "Sure."

Two hours later I leaned headfirst into the bilge of the boat, an area under the floorboards that was full of water with a greasy sheen and a strong stale smell. Peter had me holding a hose up in the air, trying to keep it from leaking water into the boat.

My skin was covered with sweat and I had a big splotch of oil on my cotton tank top. When the end of my ponytail got soaked with bilge water, I almost cried.

Peter could tell I needed a break. "Here, take this outside and see if you can get the hose clamp undone." He handed me a hose with some kind of connector on the end. When I took it, he piled more into my arms: a screwdriver, pliers, and a few other tools.

Staggering up the stairs, I started to set the parts down on the deck.

"Set up on the dock, please," Peter called up.

I climbed off the boat, then kneeled to inspect and fiddle with the hose clamp. I knew how these things worked—theoretically. But even with the right tools, the screw wasn't budging. I needed a vise.

By getting on all fours, I could hold the connector with one hand, pin the hose under my knee, and twist the screwdriver with my other hand. Sweat dripped down my chin, and my butt was sticking up in the air, jean shorts creeping up between my legs, while I strained as hard as I could against the screwdriver. I made a grunt worthy of a caveman.

A throat cleared.

I looked over my shoulder, and my upturned ass, to see a man grinning wickedly behind me. The sun was directly behind him, so I shaded my eyes to see him better. He was fair-skinned and stocky, wearing a threadbare T-shirt that accentuated his bulky shoulders and muscular arms.

"Hallo," he said, ticking up an eyebrow.

I froze, recognizing the accent. It was the man I'd seen that first day on the docks. My cheeks heated at the embarrassing—and overtly sexual—position I was in. What even was the etiquette for this situation? Shouldn't he just politely step around me and then we could both pretend this had never happened?

I sat back on my heels and looked up at him, dusting my hands off and squinting into the afternoon sun. His grin went crooked, eyes roaming over me.

"Hmm, a beautiful woman in need of some help?" His accent was soft and lilting, and my brain skipped for a moment on his words.

I glanced down at myself, at my chest sticky with sweat and starting to turn pink from too much sun, at the grit sticking to my skin, at the big splotch of oil streaked onto one boob. I looked around, just to be sure.

"Me?"

He laughed, tossing his head back. "Yes, a beautiful woman in need of some help. I am most definitely here for it." He dropped to his knees beside me and leaned in to inspect the hose clamp. "What have we here?"

I watched him, struggling with the desire to be the adventurous, independent Lila versus the Lila who wanted help, all while appreciating—in multiple ways—the bicep curled next to me.

He braced both ends against the dock and nodded at me. "Try it now."

Self-doubt won over and I tried to hand him the screwdriver. "You should do it. You're stronger."

"I have faith in you. Come on. Show it who is the boss." He winked.

I notched the screwdriver back into the head of the screw. While my assistant held the connector and hose with both hands, I bent over and twisted the tool with all of my strength.

"Almost," he encouraged.

Finally it gave, rust crackling away from the clamp. "Yes!" I shouted, throwing my hands up in the air, and he laughed with me. We both sat back and I grabbed the hem of my tank top and wiped the sweat off my face. When I looked back up, his eyes snapped from my midsection to my face.

"Thank you so much for your help."

"You are welcome." He offered me his hand. "Eivind."

"Lila." We shook.

"Well, Lila, now that I have done my knightly duties, I must move on." He mock saluted and winked. "I hope to see you again soon."

As he departed, Eivind glanced over his shoulder and busted me watching him. I blushed and gathered up the parts. But not even the prospect of helping Peter rebuild the pump could wipe the grin off my face.

Three

EDITH AND I WERE PREPARING TO WALK THE DOCKS AGAIN that evening, still hoping to find me a boat. She had returned from the trip into town and found me deep in the bilge, holding the pump and hose together while Peter tried to reconnect everything. Tools were strewn all over the boat, storage lockers emptied out, and both Peter and I were drenched in sweat. Edith had shooed me out of the boat, and as I walked down the dock to the pool, the sound of her scolding Peter faded.

I secretly hoped we would run into Eivind again, especially now that I was clean and feeling more deserving of flirting with a hot guy.

As if by fate, Edith pointed and said, "Oh, this one might be right for you. They're around your age, take on crew, and it's a beautiful boat."

My eyes roamed over the boat as we walked down the dock. *Eik* was written on the bow, and she was beautiful. The deck was open and uncluttered, and the stainless steel shone (something I'd learned takes an inordinate amount of time to polish). Instead of the rough nonskid fiberglass that some boats had, *Eik*'s deck was striped brown with thin black lines. The middle of the deck, like most boats, bulged up to accommodate the cabin, but *Eik* was low and sleek.

Edith knocked on the boat. "Jonas! Eivind!"

I perked up, and delightful bubbles of anticipation hit my stomach.

Eivind climbed out of the boat first, and he was ready with a smile for Edith, but his grin lit up even more when he saw me. "Ah, Lila, I knew you could not stay away," he crowed.

"Oh, you've met?" Edith nudged me playfully.

"Come in, come in. It is just Jonas and me here right now. The girls are at the pool."

The whos are in the what now? Those playful bubbles popped with a sour taste.

I followed behind Edith as we climbed into *Eik*'s cockpit and I hid my disappointment over a potential girlfriend. Another man climbed up out of the boat, obviously related to Eivind: they had the same strong jawline, fair skin, and bright blue eyes. Where Eivind was stacked with drool-inducing muscles, Jonas, who introduced himself as Jonas with a *J*, was taller and leaner. His hair was long and curled around the edges, a contrast to Eivind's close-cropped blond cut.

"How did your project turn out?" Eivind asked me as we settled into the bench seats around the cockpit.

"That was the end of my hard work, thankfully. Peter got the pump back in working order, and I suspect I didn't have a whole lot to do with it."

"You were very helpful, dear." Edith patted my knee. "Speaking of which, Lila here is looking to be a linehandler through the canal. Do you have your date yet?"

Jonas shook his head and focused his attention on me. "No, but the agent comes tomorrow. I was going to hire a linehandler through him." Eivind nudged Jonas. "But you could save us some money," Jonas finished with a smile.

"Right." I nodded. "And I can cook and clean, too. But I don't know much about, like, knots or anything . . . seamanship . . . stuff."

"I can teach her what she needs to know," Edith assured them.

"That is okay," Jonas said. "Marcella and Elayna know what to do, and you will most likely just be along for the ride."

"A warm body," I agreed.

"You should come by tomorrow morning. You can meet the rest of our crew and then the agent, Robert, will come in the afternoon to give us the details."

We made plans for me to swing by after breakfast the next day, and Edith and I departed.

Down the dock, I did a little jig next to Edith and sang, "I'm going to find a boat, I'm going to find a boat."

We laughed and bumped hips. I threw a last glance over my shoulder, and Eivind was on the bow of *Eik*, holding on to the rigging and watching us walk away.

When we got back to *Silver Lining*, Peter was nearly done cooking dinner. I collapsed dramatically onto the couch.

"He's so cute."

"I know, that whole boat. Everyone's so young and good-looking, it makes me wish I were decades younger."

I lifted my head up. "Those guys would be chuffed to have you, I'm sure."

Edith barked a laugh. "I hate to say it, dear, but I think maybe he's got a partner," she said while pouring herself another beer.

I sat up straight. "Really? He was so flirty."

She held out her hands, palms up. "Maybe I'm wrong. You two would be a gorgeous couple, in my humble opinion."

"Aw, thanks. Well, maybe he's single, maybe he isn't. Either way, I can't wait for tomorrow."

Whether Eivind was available or not, I reminded myself that this trip wasn't about having a fling. A fling would just be a momentary distraction, and I wasn't going to let anything disrupt my plans.

I LAY IN BED THE NEXT MORNING, THINKING ABOUT MY new possibilities. If *Eik* worked out, I would accomplish what I came here to do—transit the canal. I couldn't help but think of Eivind, too. He was very good-looking, and I could already tell he was a flirt. But my first priority was to transit the canal—not get into shenanigans with a hot sailor.

Not counting my chickens before they hatched, I still announced on the morning net that I was available to crew.

After the net, I walked down the dock to *Eik* and along the side pier. A figure stood in the cockpit, and he poked his head around the canvas when I called good morning. Mouth full and toast waving in the air, Jonas gestured to me to come in.

I picked my way around to the cockpit and climbed down onto a seat. Jonas swallowed his bite of brekkie and wished me a god morgen. People rustled around downstairs in the cabin and the scents of butter browning and sticky jam wafted out.

I settled into a cushion on the seat. "So, where did you sail from to get here?"

He swallowed the last bite of his toast and told me about the trip from Grenada. It took six days for *Eik* to sail over.

"Beautiful spinnaker sailing," Jonas said.

I made a mental note to ask Peter and Edith what a spinnaker was.

At one point, Eivind's head came up, followed by his arm and a plate with two pieces of sliced bread. "God morgen, Lila. Toast? Coffee?"

"Oh, coffee, please, and thank you. I already ate."

Eivind shrugged and set the plate down on the table. He disappeared back into the boat to return a few moments later with a jar of jam and a knife.

"Hey!" a lightly accented voice called out from below. "Thief! That's my jam."

"My boat, my jam," said Eivind. He sat across from me and tucked into his brekkie.

A woman walked up the stairs holding another plate with a piece of toast and some cut-up fruit. She put her free hand on her hip. "It is not your boat."

Eivind smirked at her. "Then it is not my jam."

The woman huffed at Eivind and used her free hand to ruffle what little hair Eivind had. She sat down next to him cross-legged and put her plate in her lap. "Who is this?"

"Lila, Marcella. Marcella, Lila."

Marcella was leggy and older than the rest of us. Her tanned skin and light accent led me to guess she came from Italy or Spain.

As Marcella dug into her breakfast, Jonas set aside his plate and turned to face me.

"So, the canal."

I clasped my hands together in front of me. "Yes."

"As you know, we need five people total; the captain, which is me, and four linehandlers, *ja*?"

I nodded. I'd read what to expect online in blog posts, so this information was not new.

"We will discuss the configurations today with the officials," he went on, "and we will be assigned a date soon. It is a two-day trip, and you would be departing from our boat in La Playita Marina on the other side of the canal. This is good?"

"Yes, so far so good. Will you want me to chip in for food?"

Jonas waved the question away. "For one night, it is fine."

"I can cook? I know you have to feed the canal officer dinner."

Jonas gestured his mug toward Marcella before taking a sip. "Marcella is our chef—and a professional— so she cooks all our meals."

Around a mouthful of brekkie, Marcella interjected, "You can clean, though."

"Of course. Where will I sleep?" I eyed the cushions around the cockpit. Sometimes the linehandlers—even the professional ones—slept out in the cockpit at night.

"Yes, where is she going to sleep?" Eivind cocked his head at his brother.

Jonas cleared his throat. "She will sleep in the crew cabin with Marcella."

Eivind and Marcella exchanged looks I couldn't read. "Then where will Elayna sleep?"

"She'll stay in my cabin." Jonas avoided meeting his brother's gaze, and Marcella watched the two carefully. When neither took the conversation further, Marcella ignored them and smiled at me. "We have bunk beds, like a slumber party."

I set my mug down. "Okay, hold on. Jonas and Elayna are . . ." There was a lot of avoiding eye contact and squirming, while Eivind smirked at Marcella. "Complicated?"

"Ah . . . yes," Jonas confirmed.

I turned to Eivind and Marcella. "What about you two?"

The smug smile on Eivind's face slipped to mock horror. "Ew."

Marcella gasped as Jonas rolled his eyes. "Ew? You would be lucky to have me, you *idiota!*" She pinched his side.

"You're old enough to be my mother, *heks!*"

Jonas calmly leaned back and drank his coffee. I leaned over to him. "What does *heks* mean?"

"'Witch.'"

When the sibling-like banter dissolved to hair pulling—on Eivind's part—Jonas gently chided his brother.

Eivind straightened and grinned at me. "The most important point is, I am single."

"Stop flirting with our new crew member, Eivind," Jonas said.

Four

EIVIND GRINNED AND RAISED AN EYEBROW. I BIT MY LIP. I opened my mouth to feed the fire, but then Jonas's words sank in.

"Wait, I'm your new crew member? Really? Even if you don't know me yet?"

Beside me, Jonas shrugged. "Marcella has been a crew member for two months. We accepted her after hanging out only a few times. You, you will be here for one night. We probably will not need you to do anything."

"Oh. Well, that's true." Four linehandlers were required, but the position of the boat might mean only two of the linehandlers would be needed—or none. I told myself that wasn't a bad thing. It meant I wouldn't accidentally screw anything up and would still be able to transit the canal.

"We are lucky to have Marcella. She is overworked and underpaid," Jonas said.

Marcella smiled at his teasing. "These boys would have starved without me."

"I can cook!" Eivind protested.

"No." Marcella slashed her hand in the air and laughed. "When I first came aboard, you had cans of Spam. When I threw them out, Elayna cried from relief."

I wrinkled my nose. "What did you make with Spam?"

Eivind leaned forward. "I have this great recipe called—"

Marcella cut him off. "Spamaroni. Eivind, darling, it was Spam and cheese and pasta. Where are the vegetables?"

"But it was so tasty!"

"See, Lila, this is why this boat needs me. Without me, they will arrive in Polynesia with scurvy."

I laughed and Eivind rolled his eyes. "Lila, I will make my Spamaroni for you. It will be the best dish you have ever put in your mouth. You will fall in love with me and declare my cooking much better than—oof!" Marcella jabbed Eivind with her elbow.

"I am sure the Spamaroni is tasty," I assured Eivind. "But I think I'm with Marcella on the vegetables. It'll take a little more greens to make me fall in love with you."

"Noted." Eivind winked again, and my stomach flipped.

"What did you do before joining *Eik*, then?" I asked Marcella. "You were a chef?"

"We met in Antigua, where I worked on a private yacht as a chef. I am from Italy, and the owners liked my cooking style, my dishes from Campania, where I grew up." She shrugged modestly.

"Sounds like a dream job. Why did you leave that boat?"

"It sounds glamorous, yes, but in reality, the owners were rarely there. Most of the time we catered to charter clients. But on that yacht, we didn't have many bookings, and I was only cooking for the crew. It was frustrating. When I left the restaurant industry, I envisioned quiet evenings making meals for the owners or for their small dinner parties while exploring the islands." She shook her head sadly. "Toward the end, I didn't feel like my food was appreciated."

"We appreciate your food," Eivind said.

"Yes, but you will eat anything I put in front of you." She poked his stomach. "Your belly and I get along quite well. Plus," she continued, turning back to me, "the big benefit was supposed to be traveling around the islands. We never left Antigua!"

"My stomach will like you just fine too," I said.

"Don't get your hopes up too much," Jonas said. "Our budget is not even close to what Marcella worked with before."

"But even my cheap meals are delicious," Marcella countered.

"Of course. I have more refined tastes than my brother and even I know your meals are delicious."

"Lila, are you on another boat?" Marcella asked me.

"Well, technically, yes. One of the boats, *Silver Lining*, has been letting me stay on board while I look for a boat to transit. I stayed in the hotel for two nights, but I have to save my money. I'm planning to backpack in South America for a few months after this."

Marcella asked me a few questions about my backpacking plans. It was hard to concentrate on her—Eivind was watching me. When our eyes met, his lips gave the cutest little quirk, the corners flicking up in pleasure.

Another person came out of the boat, interrupting a story about Brazil. This woman had dishwater-blond hair and a petite build. She loosely put a hand on Jonas's head and pulled him in to kiss his hair. Eivind's eyebrows shot up.

"Darling, please make room."

Jonas motioned to me. I slid down the seat further and he followed, while the new woman sat in the corner by the door.

Jonas leaned back a bit. "Lila, this is Elayna."

Elayna gave me a limp handshake. "*Enchanté.* Americans know this word, no?"

"Oh, I'm not American. I'm Australian."

"Oi! No worries, mate!" Eivind teased me with another wink.

I laid it on hard. "Blimey, that right there's quite the accent. You sound like you're about to pop open a stubby and wrestle a kangaroo."

Eivind laughed. "What is a stubby?"

"Why, a stubby is something you pick up from the bottle-o along with your grog so you can get smashed."

Eivind laughed harder while Jonas looked slightly horrified. "Is that English?"

I chuckled. "Yeah, but I'll take it easy on you."

Jonas eyed me. "You do sound fairly American."

"Yeah, nah, I'm Aussie, but I don't have a very strong accent."

Jonas looked more confused. "Yes, no?"

"What?"

"You said 'yeah, nah,' you are from Australia," Jonas explained.

I blushed. "Oops. Yeah, that's complicated to explain. It's, like, yeah, I know I don't have much of an Aussie accent, but no, in fact, I am not from America."

Jonas stared at me.

"Yeah, not many non-Aussies understand it either," I added.

Awkward silence.

"So, Elayna," I said, changing the topic, "how long have you been on the boat?"

"I have been on the boat since early November." Her thick French accent made her *h*'s disappear.

"Elayna found us by walking the docks in the Canaries," Jonas said, "like you are doing here."

"Oh?" I said. "You went to the Canaries to find a boat to join?"

"Well, I had a boat lined up," Elayna started. "I found its owner on a website to match boats and crew. When I arrived, it was a mess. The boat was dirty and the captain drank too much. I started to look for a different boat, and then *Eik* came in." Elayna beamed at Jonas.

Eivind rolled his eyes and he and Marcella shared a look.

Elayna turned to me. "Will you be sailing across the Pacific with us?"

"Oh, no," I said. "I'm just crewing across the canal. Speaking of which, do you have a date for the transit yet?"

Jonas shook his head. "When Robert comes by this afternoon, he'll bring a guy he calls an admeasurer." He pronounced the word slowly.

"What is an admeasurer?" Marcella asked, and I was grateful not to be the only one learning something new, at least until I realized Marcella was looking at me. I guess as the only native English speaker, I was expected to know.

I shrugged. "I have no idea. I've never heard the word before."

Jonas spoke up. "Robert says he measures the boats and we have to complete some paperwork. He is the person who will give us the transit date."

Eivind swallowed his last bite of toast and dusted off his hands. "It is fun to talk to you, Lila, but I have projects to get started on."

Our little group broke up. The crew all had their own projects to tackle: Marcella left to inventory the galley, Elayna packed up a laptop and went to the lounge to download and research some of their future ports,

Eivind had to pickle the watermaker—whatever the hell that meant—and Jonas, who worked remotely on a contract basis, had assignments to catch up on.

I excused myself and promised to be back in the afternoon to meet the agent.

Five

I KNOCKED ON THE HULL OF *EIK* AND A FACE POPPED INTO the nearby window. Elayna waved me on board. I climbed into the cockpit and Eivind met me on the stairs.

"Our agent is not here yet, but come in."

He turned and I followed him down the steep stairs into the main salon of the boat.

This was *completely* different from *Silver Lining.* The forward-facing windows let in a huge amount of light, showing me a big round table off to the left and a small couch to the right. The fabric was a deep blue and made of soft material, unlike the couches on *Silver Lining*, which were just as hard as my mattress.

"Wow. This is amazing. What kind of a boat is this?"

"*Eik* is an Oyster 56."

Not that it meant anything to me.

Jonas sat working on his laptop at a desk to my far right. Both women were in the galley around the corner to my left.

Eivind led me forward on the boat to a small hallway. An open door on the left side showed me a small cabin with two bunk beds. The bottom bunk was neatly made and free of clutter. The messier top bunk contained some books and headphones.

The mattresses were tapered, with the narrow end toward the front of the boat. There was room for a small set of cabinets for clothes and whatnot. I couldn't help myself; I pressed on the mattress and sighed in relief when the memory foam squished underneath the sheet.

"You'll share this room with Marcella. She has the top bunk and you'll take the bottom."

"Is it weird that I'm kicking Elayna out of her room?"

Eivind chuckled. He leaned in and whispered, "I do not think either of them will suffer too much." His eyebrows waggled and my cheeks heated.

He turned around and put his hand on the door across the hall. "This is the head. You have been using the restrooms at the marina, yes?"

"Yes."

"Same here. But when we leave the dock to do the transit, we will start using our heads again. Let me show you, and if you need a refresher when you move in, ask, ja?"

The head was very small, so I had to lean in from the hallway while Eivind very matter-of-factly showed me how to use the toilet. Only bodily fluids and toilet paper went into the bowl. He pressed and held a button to fill the bowl with water, then pressed and held another button to flush. The flush was loud, sucking the water down with violence.

"Nothing else goes in the toilet. We have a little bin for female products here." He opened a cabinet under the sink where there was a small bin with a liner. Extra toilet paper and some cleaning supplies were stacked up on one side. "If you need to clean up, it is all in there. If you take a shit, you will want to flush two or three times, to get it out of the pipes and make sure the toilet is clean for the next person, okay?"

"No worries."

"Good. Any questions, let me know. One of the joys of cruising is that occasionally we all have to deal with our literal shit together." Eivind grinned.

"Oh God, I bet there are great stories."

Eivind knocked on the wall behind the toilet. "Here there is a holding tank. For all the waste. Before that, it goes through a . . . pump." Eivind mimed a tumbling motion with his fingers. "To, err . . . blend it. Like a frozen drink."

I groaned. "Thanks, you've put me off daiquiris."

"Once, the tank clogged, so it was full of shit. And Jonas had to shove a wire up from the outside to unclog it and he could not push himself away fast enough and . . ." Eivind blew a raspberry.

"Wow. Poor Jonas."

Eivind grinned again and shrugged. Stepping out of the head, he closed the door. "Welcome to cruising life."

A knock sounded from up on the deck and Jonas went to check it out. Soon he climbed back in with two men in tow: a beefy guy, dark skinned and older; the other a short Asian man. Introductions were made between us and Robert, the agent, and Hiro, the admeasurer, and we all crammed around the table. Eivind pressed in next to me, our thighs touching.

Jonas started filling out paperwork while Robert collected the passports of the other crew and asked Jonas questions. Jonas wrote in neat block handwriting and still managed to keep up with the conversation. I tried to follow as best I could while they discussed the specifications of the boat, but details like horsepower and fenders and moorings went over my head.

At one point we all moved outside and Hiro measured the boat. He had an actual tape measure. Marcella stood at the bow and held one end of the tape measure while he walked down the dock. He marked the distance to one of the metal rails, and we all got back on board and he did the same thing, handing Jonas the tape measure to hold while he walked down the back of the boat.

Eik's stern extended past the dock, so Hiro finished measuring the boat by leaning over the rail and using his arm span to hold the measuring tape all the way to the end—the far edge of *Eik*'s dinghy.

"Fifty-seven feet, three inches," he pronounced.

We went back inside for more discussion. Hiro showed us how the boats could go through the canal.

"You have three choices," he said, flipping a piece of paper over to the blank side and slashing his pen across to divide it into three sections. "A row by yourself, a raft-up in the middle of the row, or tied to a bigger ship."

Sailboats were the bottom of the barrel. The canal authorities would put a big ship—a cruise ship or cargo ship—in the canal, and then, if there was room, a row or two of sailboats could go in in front or behind the big ship.

"Option one," Hiro said, "you go by yourself." He sketched a little oval in the middle of the top section and drew lines from the four "corners" of the oval outward. "This is more work. You have all four linehandlers working here." He tapped his pen on the page, marking *Eik*'s four corners.

"If you do this," Robert interrupted, "you should hire professional linehandlers from me. It is a lot harder to control the boats, and my men are experienced."

"Option two," Hiro continued, "you raft up with other sailboats." In the second section, Hiro drew four ovals across the center and made the lines to the corners again, except this time the lines only extended from the two outside boats. "We tie the boats together and only two crew on the outside boats have to manage the lines.

"Option three. We have the wall on this side." Hiro pointed. "A small ship—a cruise ship, tugboat, etcetera—ties up to the wall, and we tie sailboats up to it." He drew a big box against the wall, with little ovals next to it. "This is the best one. The small ship goes through a lot, their crew are professionals, they manage the lines. It's very easy for you. What do you want to do?"

"You can also opt to take the first available," Robert said. "If you are in a hurry."

Jonas and Eivind looked at each other.

"First available," Jonas said.

"Ja," Eivind agreed.

With that decision made, Hiro packed up the paperwork. "I'll give Robert your transit times as soon as I have them," he said, before shaking our hands and departing.

Robert stayed behind to talk about some more formalities with Jonas, and Eivind kept a close ear on the conversation and chimed in. Marcella and Elayna wandered off to their room, but I stayed on the couch, pressed into Eivind. Neither of us moved.

That was how I saw the bill for hiring an agent and transiting the canal. Jonas had paid several thousand dollars to sail through. I could only imagine how much money the big ships spent. But what choice did they have? The alternative, Jonas told me, would be to sail around Cape Horn, which was notorious for wild seas and cold weather.

Finally Robert said his goodbyes and left. Marcella and Elayna came out of their cabins dressed in bathers and left for the pool. Jonas settled into the kitchen, putting away dishes. Eivind shifted over and hiked his leg up onto the couch, his knee touching my hip.

"Lila, do you know how to be a linehandler?"

Six

EIVIND LED ME OUT TO THE DECK OF THE BOAT. HE grabbed a spare rope that hung off the rail and we walked to the bow.

He pointed down to a metal fixture on the deck. "This is a cleat. We have them all over the boat"—he pointed out various others—"and this is how we attach the boat to the dock or a wall or another boat. Whatever we need."

The cleat was a piece of metal in a T shape, with a short, stubby base and longer arms. The edges were all rounded and curved. Most of the cleats on the right side of the boat had ropes wrapped around them, which were tied to cleats on the dock.

"Wait here." Eivind crossed the deck and climbed down onto the dock. He went to a cleat on the dock ahead of me and to the left. Quickly, he fastened the rope to the cleat, his hand a blur of movement.

"Now I will throw you the line, yes?"

"Okay." I held my hands out like a footy player ready to catch.

"Ah, not like that. Hold your arm out like this." Eivind demonstrated, holding his arm straight out to the side of his body. "I will aim for just over your arm, and all you have to do is—" He mimed a curl, catching an invisible rope between his bicep and forearm.

"Okay." I held out my arm.

Like William Tell's son getting an apple shot off his head, I had to trust Eivind not to brain me with the line. Eivind kept the rope coiled in one hand and held some slack in the other. He swung the rope once, twice, and on the third time he let go and it flew toward me. I closed my eyes and winced, but the rope hit my arm and I quickly grabbed at it.

Eivind gave me a boyish grin. "See, I have a good aim, yes?"

I laughed. "Yes, okay. I trust you."

He nodded decisively and climbed back aboard. "Take the line over the lifelines, on the outside—yes, good—and pull the line under."

I squatted on the deck next to the cleat. "Lifelines?" I asked, placing my hand on the rail. Unlike *Silver Lining*'s, this rail was soft under my fingertips.

"Yes. They will save your life. They are to keep you from going overboard."

I inspected the lifelines skeptically, which were made of a thin rope with a fine texture. "They don't look very strong."

Eivind crouched beside me. "They are a special material called Dyneema. The boat has"—he waved his arm to encompass all of *Eik*—"so much Dyneema. It is super strong and light. That is why we use it. Trust me."

"Okay, so what do I do with the rope?"

"Line. It is called a line."

"What's the difference?"

"A line is cut a specific length; a rope is not."

"But aren't all ropes cut to a specific length? There's not a rope somewhere out there with infinite length."

Eivind rubbed the stubble on his jaw. "Yes, but the line, it has a job. It is cut to do something specifically. Like, this line is for a dock line. We use it to tie our boat to the dock. You see?"

"I think so. So, do you have any rope on board?"

Eivind chuckled. "No, I think not. It is all lines."

"Okay, so what do I do with the *line*?"

"With the *line*"—Eivind nudged me playfully—"we take it around the base of the cleat. One whole trip around and you bring the line like this . . ."

Eivind demonstrated a figure-eight shape around the two arms of the cleat. "To lock it, you make a loop and twist." He tucked the loose end of the line under one of the previous wraps. Eivind tugged it and then stood up, reaching over the lifeline to pull hard on the newly tied-off line. "That is how you cleat a line."

We undid and redid the line over and over again until I was confident, Eivind guiding my hands when I got confused, or watching me carefully to make sure I understood.

"When we go through the canal, there will be people on the walls with a thing called a monkey's fist. The monkey's fist has a small line attached, so they throw this monkey's fist at you. It usually will hit the deck and that is okay. They try not to hit the windows. You grab it and pull the small line up. This small line, you tie to our line, and they will pull our line up onto the wharf. Understand?"

I nodded, feeling heavier with the responsibility. I had to catch the monkey's fist or make sure it didn't hit the windows and then make the transfer of the line. "Okay."

"Okay. When the canal is emptying the water, the boat goes down and you have to loosen the line." Eivind demonstrated this by taking most, but not all, of the wraps off the cleat. "Hold this."

I grabbed the line while Eivind jumped back down to the dock. He wrapped a hand around the line, just above the cleat, and pulled. I walked my hands down the line, letting it out.

"Good. Not too much, you still need"—Eivind used one fist to mime pulling—"tension. I will loosen the line, like when the boat will be raised in the canal."

I gradually pulled the line in until it was tight with the cleat on the dock. I bent over to finish the figure eights and the lock on the cleat.

"Very good. So, Jonas is the captain, and he will be at the helm. If he tells you to cleat the line off, you cleat the line off, no matter what. Okay?"

"Okay, cool." I couldn't help grinning. I'd learned so much already. Eivind climbed back on board.

"What else do you want to learn?"

"I'm sure you have better things to do than teach me about boats."

Eivind's eyes held mine and he leaned into me. "No. I have nothing I want to do more than teach you about boats."

We smiled at each other for a few moments until I snapped myself out of it.

I looked around me. "Hmm . . . okay, let's start with what I do know. This is the mast." I put my hand up against the large metal column in the center of the boat. "And that thing's the boom." I pointed to the large horizontal metal thing sticking out from the mast. "Mainsail, shroud, jib?"

"Genoa. That sail is a genoa; it is bigger than a jib."

"Okay. So which of these lines do you pull to unroll the genoa?"

Eivind showed me where the lines for each sail ran, which line you pulled, which lines you released. I wasn't going sailing, but Eivind kept up with it anyway, patiently explaining.

I pointed to one thing. "What's this?"

"Hmm . . . a thingamabob?"

I laughed. "How do you know that word?"

"As a kid, Jonas obsessed over *The Little Mermaid*. Mum made us watch all the Disney movies in English for practice. In our house, we had thingamabobs and dinglehoppers when we were growing up. He always wanted to play Prince Eric with the neighbor girls who had red hair. We stayed friends with them for so long. I am pretty sure Jonas did not even like them, but they had red hair, so . . ." He shrugged.

"And you? What did you want to play when you were little?"

Eivind grinned. "I wanted to be a rock star."

"Were you in a band?"

"Yes, but we were terrible." Eivind sat down on the top of the main salon's roof, stretching his legs out on the deck in front of him.

"What did you play?" I sat down next to him and leaned back on my hands.

"Guitar."

"That's definitely the hottest instrument. I think you should play some guitar for me."

He laughed. "I do not have one here. How do you feel about a ukulele?"

I scrunched up my nose. "A ukulele is cute, not sexy."

"Ah, so if I want to seduce you, I need to borrow a guitar."

I grinned. Eivind's eyes scanned my face, dipping to look at my lips and then traveling back up to meet my eyes.

I turned my face away. Closing my eyes, I sighed and tilted my head back. The sun heated my skin. "Unless I want a sunburn, we should wrap up out here."

Eivind laughed. "Then I know what time it is." I checked my watch, which read 4:34 p.m. "Sundowners!"

It was a little earlier than I typically started drinking, but I also knew a lot of people on the dock always had a beer in hand. Eivind led me back into the boat, where we found Jonas now sitting at the table with his laptop. Eivind reached into the fridge and grabbed a beer. "Jonas, *øl*?"

"Ja."

Eivind tossed the beer at his brother. "Lila, would you like a stubby?" He grinned mischievously.

I clapped my hands to my face in mock horror. "Oh no! I led you astray. This is not a stubby. This is a tinny. A stubby is a bottle; a tinny is a can."

Eivind laughed again and I was learning to love his smile. It came easily and often. Jonas was nice, but he was more reserved than Eivind.

"I like *tinny* better. *Stubby* sounds like a stiffy." Eivind pointed to his crotch to make sure his meaning was clear, and I burst out laughing. I even caught the corner of Jonas's lip twitching up. Eivind pulled out two more beers. "Come on, let's go up top and leave my brother to his work."

Eivind handed me my beer, grabbed a bag of chips, and climbed back up to the cockpit. He settled into a cushion, leaning his back against the wall, his foot on the bench, and his knee cocked up against the side. I sat next to him, crossed my legs, and popped my beer open.

"You and your brother must be close," I said. "To go sailing together for so long."

"Yes and no. We were not close before. But now we are best friends. And that was what we wanted. Why I came."

"The boat belongs to Jonas?"

Eivind nodded. "He wanted to do this for a long time. And the timing was good for him with his work, so he bought the boat. Not many people would want to do this. He couldn't find someone to go with him, so he asked me." He shrugged. "It turned out to be a good decision. I am happy here. On *Eik*."

"What does Jonas do for work?"

"He was an engineer, but he left that job to do technical writing. He works for a scientific journal, editing and proofreading the articles."

"And what about you?"

Eivind reached over and pulled the bag of chips open, taking out a handful. "I do nothing. I am the loser brother." He smirked at me.

I reached my hand into the bag and grabbed a big chip. I pointed it at him. "I don't believe that."

"I went to university and graduated with a degree in chemistry, to be in science like my big brother. But instead I ended up working in a restaurant. So that is what I do."

I shrugged and took another chip. "After uni I worked in a call center for a few months, as a temp job, even though I have a degree in engineering. I saved up money to travel. Those jobs may be things we do now or things we do forever. I don't think my life will be all about what I do for a job, though."

Eivind winked at me. "So smart."

"The question is, what do you *want* to do?"

Eivind let his head loll back and he blinked up at the sky for a few minutes. "I am not sure."

"Really? No big dreams?" My brain had a hard time wrapping itself around the idea that someone my age wouldn't know what they wanted to do with their lives.

He laughed. "I am living in my brother's dream."

"Okay, well, do you like it?"

"I do. There are always many projects to do on the boat, and I get to work with my hands a lot more. All the systems are interesting to me, but the engine especially. We have lots of books, and do not tell Jonas, but if something were to go wrong . . ." He shrugged and grinned. "I might enjoy the challenge."

"That's kind of the hands-on side of engineering, yeah?" I nudged him. "I've got the degree, but you probably know more about engines than I do."

"What is your plan with your degree?" He leaned in closer to me.

"When I'm done with my trip, I'll be interviewing for jobs in engineering on the east coast—Sydney or Brisbane, probably. In a few years, I should be able to buy a house, and then, of course, have a family."

"That is . . . a lot of plans."

"Yeah." I sighed wistfully. "Sounds like you might like to be a tradie."

"What is a tradie?"

"An electrician or a mechanic or a plumber. Something like that. Or, I suppose, there are equivalents for marine jobs."

Eivind looked thoughtful. "I am learning a lot. Maybe so." He took a sip of his beer. "So, you have big plans. Why are you not doing those things now? Why pause your dreams to fly halfway around the world?"

"I guess . . ." I faltered. "I guess anyone can go on a vacation to an exotic destination, but what do they really get out of it? I wanted to experience something different, and prove that I could do something like this on my own." I huffed a laugh. "My mum is overprotective to a fault, and I just didn't want to be seen as *sheltered* or *spoiled* anymore."

"Someone said that?"

I bit my lip, nodded, and shrugged all at once, embarrassed.

Eivind was silent for a moment, and then he tipped his beer toward mine. "To life-changing adventures."

I tapped my tinny against his and took a sip.

"Now, let me tell you more about our dear captain . . ."

Eivind told me about growing up in Norway, the escapades that he and Jonas got into. I was surprised to learn Eivind and Jonas were ten years apart; Jonas looked a bit younger than he was and Eivind looked a bit older. Jonas's longer hair made him look unkempt, and Eivind's close-cropped hair gave him an air of maturity.

"Jonas was already older and more mature, but when our father left, he really grew up too fast. This is his playtime now. He was too busy helping our mum."

I cocked my head. "He does seem like a father figure to you. Keeping you in line," I teased. "How did this whole thing come about anyway?" I gestured to the boat.

"Ah." Eivind sat back. "Jonas is divorced. And after the divorce, he did that guy thing . . . you know, not showering and pajamas and pizza boxes. He was clicking around on the internet when he found this YouTube channel of a couple getting ready to go sailing. He invited me over one night and said, 'Look at this, people do this, we can do this, but I need you.' Because he couldn't do the boat by himself."

"Wow, that's intense." I was quiet for a moment, thinking about the brother who would ask for this and the brother who would pause his whole life to help him.

Eivind got another beer, and when he returned, he sat next to me, resting his arm on the ledge behind my back. We weren't touching, but the heat from his arm radiated toward me, the brightness of his skin wafting around me, like lemons and hops. Suddenly this yearning hit me—to be in a foreign place, on a grand adventure, with a beautiful man. It felt like I could have anything.

"Ciao!" Marcella's voice called out from the dock. She and Elayna were back from the pool and the boat quickly became a bustle of voices and activity.

"I should go," I said, and Eivind's face flashed with disappointment, but then he grinned.

"Will I see you tomorrow?"

I smirked. "I'm not going anywhere unless it's on this boat. You are stuck with me."

Eivind's eyes dipped to my lips briefly, but he let me go. "Tomorrow."

Seven

WHEN I FLOUNCED DOWN INTO *SILVER LINING*, PETER and Edith were sitting around the dining room table.

"He's *single*!" I sang. "Oh, and also," I said nonchalantly, "I'm going through the canal."

"Good job, dear," Edith said. "I don't know which to ask about first."

I laughed. "Well, Jonas is with Elayna, one of the girls. Eivind is single."

"Ah." Edith rested her chin on her fist. "They are both attractive, don't get me wrong, but Jonas is more my type. His hair, his eyes . . ."

Peter cleared his throat.

"Right, on to point two. Are you going through the canal with *Eik*, then?"

"Yes, we talked over all the particulars, and I have been given the stamp of approval."

"Congratulations, dear." Edith checked her watch. "This calls for celebratory sundowners."

Edith and I faffed about in the galley, pouring drinks and putting together a plate of nibbles. We reconvened back up top in the cockpit, where Edith sat down and leaned towards me with a conspiratorial look.

"So, what are you going to do about Eivind?"

My eyes lost focus as I thought about all the things I'd *like* to do.

"Oh, Lila." She giggled and swatted at me. "Your face. Please, I don't want to know what *that* thought was."

I blushed. "What? He's very good-looking."

"He is," she agreed.

I sobered up and wrinkled my nose at Edith. "It's probably not a good idea to start anything with him, right?"

"Why do you say that?"

"Well, if we hooked up, there's so much that could go wrong. Maybe I like him too much, maybe he likes me too much, or maybe we'd just be awful together."

Edith snorted. "Based on the chemistry I've seen, I doubt that will happen."

I laughed. "I know. But if it crashed and burned, maybe they wouldn't want me on the boat anymore, or maybe I'd go and it would be all awkward."

"Ah, I see. I know going through the canal is really important to you, so I understand how it might be better not to risk it—for now."

"Yeah. Argh, Edith." I let my head fall back and I flopped my arms out dramatically. "Why must you be so mature and wise? Why can't you just tell me to enjoy life and fling my wild oats while I'm young?"

"Years of experience," she said dryly.

"Yeah, no, you are right. Starting something with Eivind may not be the best."

"But you know, there's a light at the end of the tunnel. I bet you can work it out to have at least a night of fun over in Panama City." She grinned cheekily.

"The whole thing feels a bit like star-crossed lovers. Now I only want him more." I bit back a grin.

Edith whacked me with a pillow.

———————

THE NEXT DAY, I SAT IN THE SALON OF *SILVER LINING* AND was having lunch with Peter and Edith when Eivind called on the radio.

"*Silver Lining, Silver Lining*, this is *Eik*."

I looked at Peter, and he motioned to the radio. "Well, go get it." I picked up the microphone and pressed the talk button. "*Silver Lining* here. Go ahead, *Eik*."

"One seven?" Eivind was asking to switch to another channel to have a longer conversation.

"One seven." I turned the knob on the radio to change it to channel seventeen and waited for Eivind.

"*Eik* here, Lila?"

"Hey, Eivind," I said.

"I wanted to let you know we have been assigned our transit date. It is March first. We have also cleaned up the cabins, and you can come to stay on *Eik*."

My heart sank. This was later than I had hoped for. My flight to leave Panama departed on the second. I could not do the transit and make my flight; we would need all day both days to complete our transit through the canal. "That's great news, Eivind. Let me get back to you about the cabin, okay?"

"Okay, come by anytime. *Eik* standing by on seven-four."

"*Silver Lining* back to seven-four."

"Why the long face, bub?" Edith asked.

"My flight is on March second. I would have to change it."

"Can you do that?"

"I don't know. I have to look at the policy. But it's not just changing my flight. I'd planned out three months total, with the first three weeks here. If I extend my stay in Panama, I'd have to cut something out."

"How important is it to you to go through the canal?"

I sighed and massaged my forehead. "I was really excited. I *am* really excited."

Edith nodded. "Go look into the fees for changing your flight. No sense in getting too worked up about it if you lose all your money or something."

"Good point." I grabbed my phone, waved bye, and headed to the pool to use the Wi-Fi.

I sat in a chair under an umbrella and pulled up my flight details to look for the rebooking policy. I could rebook my flight for $250, and the cheapest flight was on March 7. I did some quick math; by staying on *Silver Lining*, I'd only stayed two nights at the hotel, and I would have to pay for a few nights once I got back to Panama City. I knew the rates for the hostels in the area and there were some cheap places, though they weren't in the best areas. I had wanted to stay in the Casco Viejo, but a once-in-a-lifetime experience would be worth it, right?

I winced as I tapped the confirm button, but I tried to mentally refocus myself on the canal. I had a boat to hitchhike on, and I was one step closer to achieving my goal.

BACK ON *SILVER LINING*, I ASKED EDITH IF I COULD STAY A few more days with them until *Eik* left.

"Of course, dear. But don't you want to move over to *Eik*?"

We sat in the cockpit, having wraps for lunch.

"Yeah, nah. I would prefer to stay here if you'll have me."

Edith gave me a pointed look. "What about the young man? Eivind?"

"What about him?"

"Don't give me that innocent face. You get all happy and dreamy every time you mention him."

I swallowed the last bite of my wrap. "Nothing's going to happen with Eivind. I don't want things to be awkward."

Edith nodded sagely. "Good plan—avoid him instead. Keep him on his toes."

I rolled my eyes. "I know it's not a great plan." I flopped onto my back. "He's just so . . ."

"You could climb him like a tree."

I quirked an eyebrow at her.

"I think that's what the kids are calling it these days."

"In Straya we would say 'rooting.'" I wrinkled my forehead. "I wonder why we have all the plant metaphors."

"Whichever plant metaphor you go with, what is going on with Eivind?"

"Nothing. How can there be? He'll be out of my life when we get to Panama City."

"I would think a young woman as adventurous as you would be open to meeting an exotic lover"—she waggled her eyebrows—"while traveling."

I startled and looked up at Edith. "You think I'm adventurous?"

"Of course. It's not every day you meet someone who takes as big a leap as you have."

I smiled, pleased.

Edith changed the subject. "Have you called your mother and told her you found a boat?"

I groaned and covered my face with a pillow. "I'll call my dad tonight."

"Are you avoiding your mom?"

I pulled the pillow back. "Let's say I'm avoiding negative energy. Nobody needs that in their life."

Edith looked at me skeptically.

"Dad's easier to share this stuff with. Mum is so mad right now. She's never been much for adventure, so . . ." I shrugged.

"Speaking as a mother, I can see how it's tough for her. What about your dad makes him so supportive?"

"Well, that was the magic of the Panama Canal. Dad's a drafter by trade, and he's always been a bit obsessed with the 'engineering marvels.' That's why I studied engineering—Dad was always talking about it. So I told them I was going to see the canal up close and personal, and he was totally on board. He's going to be so excited for me. And that's what I need."

I WAITED UNTIL DAD WAS AT WORK BEFORE I CALLED.

"Sweet pea!" he jovially answered the phone.

"Hey, Dad! How's your workday going?"

"It's just fine here. Let me get this out of the way: your mother would like a phone call soon."

I sighed. "I know. I will call her, just not yet. But for now, I have good news. I found a boat!"

"Hey, that's great! Tell me about it."

I told my dad all about *Eik*, the two brothers, and my lessons in lines and other boat knowledge.

"You'll be joining a boat with two men on board? How old are they?"

"It's not just Eivind and Jonas; there are two women as well: Elayna and Marcella."

"Ah okay. Maybe lead with that when you tell your mum about it, okay?"

"Good plan."

"How old are they?"

I rolled my eyes. "Eivind's my age. Jonas is a bit older."

The silent pause made me picture my dad frowning at me. "I suppose I shouldn't wish for them to be mean. Are they at least ugly?"

"Dad!"

"So no?"

"Devilishly handsome."

"Dang it."

"I'll be fine. It's only for one night and then I'll move on. I'm not looking to get involved with anyone." I changed the subject. "Did you finish that miniseries you were watching?"

"I did! Did you know that some people estimate the death toll for the workers building the canal at twenty-five thousand?"

"No, I didn't."

I leaned back on my bed, letting Dad tell me all the interesting facts he'd learned. When I'd told him my plan to transit the canal, he'd been so excited for me, helping me pitch it to Mum as an "educational adventure."

Part of what intrigued me so much about this adventure was living it for my dad, and his excitement bubbling up through the phone made it more real to me.

Eight

THE NEXT DAY, IN THE LATE AFTERNOON HEAT, I SAT BY the pool reading. Peter had some new project he had to work on, and Edith had quickly hustled me out of the boat and toward the pool before I could be recruited.

The antithesis of hard work was lounging by the pool, so that was where I went. Neither my accommodations nor the pool facilities were luxurious, but I tried to make the best of it. I had time on my hands to relax and read, plus I had an esky full of tinnies to drink. As nice as a fruity daiquiri would have been, I couldn't afford it.

I'd been out for half an hour when a voice called my name.

"Hello, Lila!" The crew of *Eik* walked toward me, dressed down in bathers and thongs.

"Hey there!" They claimed the chairs around me. After dropping their stuff off and exchanging pleasantries, Marcella, Elayna, and Jonas stepped down into the pool.

Eivind had stretched out on the chair to my right, kicking his thongs off and lowering the back of his lounger. He turned his head and smiled at me. I was close enough that I could see his eyes behind his sunnies, and I watched as he checked me out from head to toe.

My curly hair was up in a messy bun on top of my head, and I'd only packed one bather, a red string bikini that gave me plenty of coverage but no support—not that I needed much.

I couldn't be affronted about being so openly scoped. I ogled Eivind too. He wore short trunks, showing off his chest and legs. My first impression had been right: Eivind's shoulders were broad, his arms and abs muscled and bulky.

He bent the knee closest to me and met my eye. We grinned at each other in mutual appreciation.

I put my e-reader down beside me. "No swimming for you?"

"Nah, I would rather sit here for a little while."

"I like to work up a sweat a bit, sitting in the heat, and then take a dip."

"Back home we do the opposite, in hot springs. When I was a child, Jonas and I used to sit out in the snow until we could not stand it anymore, and then we'd hop into the hot water."

"How old were you?"

Eivind scratched his chest. "I must have been seven or eight?" He was silent for a moment. "Now that I think about it, Jonas must have been letting me win. He would have been seventeen or eighteen. There is no way I could have lasted longer than he did out there."

"Aw, that's cute."

Eivind smiled softly.

I held up my sunscreen bottle. "Hey, can you put some on my back? I need to flip over to even out my tan."

"Sure." Eivind grabbed the bottle while I twisted away from him. I gathered the wispy hairs from the back of my neck and held them up out of the way.

Eivind slopped some sunscreen onto my back and focused on rubbing it in. He was thorough. Very thorough, sweeping his hand under the strings of my bikini. So thorough that before long I was giggling.

"All right, handsy, you got everything."

He chuckled and handed me the bottle. "I am just concerned about your skin health. If you sunburn, let me know and I will come over and rub some aloe on you too."

I snorted and adjusted my chair all the way down, then flipped onto my stomach. Eivind did the same, and we lay facing each other.

We talked about our days; I told Eivind about the project I'd been helping Peter with, and he told me about working on the watermaker with Jonas.

We were interrupted by Elayna approaching, dripping wet, and asking for Eivind's help finding a pool toy they'd stuffed into one of the bags with the towels and beers. She stood off to the side, dripping onto the concrete while Eivind's dry hands dug through the bags.

"Lila, would you like to come play? It is a game of keep-up."

"Yeah, that sounds fun. I'm breaking a sweat here anyway. Eivind, you want to play?"

He shook his head and sat up. "Thank you, but I will watch only."

He twisted around to fiddle with the lounge chair while I followed Elayna into the pool. As I stepped in, the water cooled my sun-kissed skin.

It took me a little while to get into the game; I was distracted by Eivind's eyes constantly watching me. He wasn't helping the situation or being shy about it. Every time I glanced over, he grinned at me and I blushed.

Eventually I focused, and the four of us passed the ball back and forth, setting it like a volleyball. We didn't keep score, just passed to whomever we wanted and tried not to let it touch the water. Jonas, with his long limbs, made some good last-minute saves.

We wore ourselves out and retreated to the shade. Once dry, I asked Eivind to reapply the sunscreen—which he enthusiastically did. Elayna and Marcella grabbed their pool noodles and returned to the water, while Jonas sat on my other side.

My lounger had been pulled slightly closer to Eivind's than it had been before I went in the water.

"Jonas, what does *Eik* mean?"

"*Eik* means 'oak,' like the tree, in Norwegian. The Vikings built their boats out of oak because it is strong and flexible. Although *Eik* is not made of wood, she is strong." He smiled.

"How long have you owned the boat? And where did you start?"

Jonas told me about buying the boat in England the previous year. He bought it nearly new. Someone had ordered it from the factory, launched it, and then had to sell it due to an issue with their job.

"That's insane," I said. "I can't imagine spending all that time and money only to have to give up your dream."

We traded stories for a while, talking about home. Jonas relaxed more than I'd seen him before, happy and stretched out in the sun. He smiled more, and I wondered what had changed.

In contrast, Eivind was quieter, happy to listen to his brother's chatter.

In the pool, Marcella and Elayna bobbed in the water, whispering to each other in low voices, and occasionally stealing glimpses of Jonas, who was oblivious.

A light touch on my arm brought my attention back to Eivind.

"If I swim, will you come?"

Sweat dripped down my elbows. "Yes, that sounds lovely."

Eivind and I stepped into the pool, and I felt a little bad that we had invaded the girls' space. They smiled at us, but after a few moments, they climbed out of the pool to dry off.

Eivind and I were alone. There were other people in the loungers on the deck, but it was still pretty quiet around the pool. The sun started to duck behind the buildings, and shade crept over the concrete.

We sighed in pleasure at the cool water.

"Jonas seems different today," I remarked.

Eivind nodded. "Yes, it takes some time to unwind from a passage. The responsibility for us all falls on him, so it is hard on him."

I hummed and leaned back against the wall, thinking about what it must be like to captain your own boat. We bobbed in silence. Suddenly Eivind took a deep breath and sunk down into the water. I stood up and watched from the surface as he cycled his arms and legs, keeping himself down at the bottom.

And I waited.

And waited.

I chewed my lip. I could see him pretty clearly down at the bottom, and he didn't look panicked. I've been told since I was a child, though, that drowning doesn't look like drowning, and to reassure myself, I reached down and tugged his arm. He stood up, surfacing and wiping the water off his face.

"How do you do that?" I asked.

"Hold my breath for that long?"

I nodded.

He leaned in. "I will tell you my secrets."

Eivind taught me how to do some breathing exercises and had me float on my back, his palms lifting me up. "Breathe in," he coached, "and out." We breathed together for several minutes. He told me it was all about relaxing and thinking about something else.

On his cue, I emptied my lungs of air and then refilled them deeply. We sunk to the bottom together, sitting cross-legged on the floor of the pool, peddling our arms to stay down. To distract myself, I looked right at Eivind—and immediately laughed all my air out.

I broke the surface, panting, and Eivind popped up again. "Okay," I sputtered. "You can't look at me while I do this!"

He tossed his head back and laughed, gathering me up into his arms. "Okay, okay. Try again."

I leaned back into his arms, a little bit closer to his body this time. I closed my eyes as I breathed in rhythm with his voice.

On our next deep inhale, we went down again. Eivind arranged our knees to touch as we sat on the floor. I looked at him and found his eyes closed. He looked transcendental in his calm, even with his arms swirling and keeping him down.

I distracted myself by studying his face: the strong jaw, the slight stubble, the narrowing to his chin. With his eyes closed, without the view of those startlingly blue eyes, I focused on his mouth. I tried to ignore the burn of my lungs and focus on those soft pink lips, but as distracting as they were, I couldn't take it anymore.

As I rose to the surface, Eivind came up after me.

"Very good!" he exclaimed.

"How long did I last?"

He screwed up his face in thought. "Thirty seconds?"

"What? That's it?"

He laughed. "If you want, next time I can bring weights to sink us to the bottom. It makes it easier to stay down."

I grinned at him. "Yeah, let's do that."

We practiced several more times, and Marcella eventually joined us, standing by the rim and using a phone as a stopwatch. I got up to forty-five seconds once.

When we tired of the pool, we hopped out and basked in the sun to dry off. The light was fading, the shadows growing longer, until the lights around the pool clicked on. We gathered our things, and Jonas invited me back to *Eik* for a sundowner.

Walking down the dock, we found a party going on at one of the sailboats. I'd had sundowners with this couple before. In their late fifties, Fred was tall and athletic with a nose that had been broken once or twice, and Poppy was an energetic and lithe retired schoolteacher. They were a hoot, gregarious and generous.

They were enjoying the cooler evening with a few neighbors I didn't know as well. The six of them crowded around their cockpit table, drinking and laughing as we approached.

As soon as Poppy spotted me, her eyes lit up, and she waved us on board. We all climbed into the seats, the eleven of us making it a tight fit. Fred passed out tinnies, one of the men asked Jonas about his watermaker project, and Poppy sidled up next to me.

She squeezed my shoulders. "I'm so glad you found a boat to crew on! We would have taken you, of course, but with this engine issue, we just don't know when we will be able to go through."

"I know, no worries. And I think it's gonna work out well on *Eik*," I said.

We chatted about a few other things, Poppy filling me in on her trip to Panama City a few days earlier. She'd asked on the VHF net for a dentist recommendation, so I knew she'd gone in to have a crown replaced.

Breaking off her thought, she leaned into me. "Girlfriend, *what* is going on with Eivind?"

I blushed. "What?"

She scoffed and shimmied her shoulder against mine. "Don't act all innocent. He keeps looking at you."

I glanced across the room, and Eivind's eyes caught mine. We grinned at each other. I glanced back at Poppy, who looked at me smugly.

"Yup."

I laughed. "Yeah, nah. Nothing yet. He's been great, though. He's teaching me a lot of boat stuff, and today we did some free diving in the pool."

"What did he teach you on the boat?"

I told her about our lessons and some of the sailing terminology I had added to my vocabulary.

"Has he shown you how to tie a bowline?" she asked me.

I shook my head.

She set her drink down and clapped her hands. "I'll teach you! I have a fun way to learn it. Come on!"

Poppy led me up onto the bow of the boat, opened one of the lockers, and grabbed a small line for our practice.

"The bowline is one of the most important knots to learn," she told me, sounding like the former teacher. "It makes a strong loop at one end of the line, and sailors all practice till they can do it quick and easy."

She showed me how to hold the line and loop one side of it. "Now the rabbit comes out of the hole," she said, "around the tree, and back in the hole." She pulled her hands apart and showed me the tidy and tight loop. "You try."

I made the rabbit run its lap a few times until I got the hang of it.

"Here's how you can tell if you've done the knot right." She held the line in front of her hips, the loop dangling down on her thighs. The end of the line stuck straight out of the knot, pointing towards me. "It's a boy knot."

I burst out laughing, and Poppy grinned at me. I practiced a few more times, and then she showed me how to tie the knot with one hand behind my back. Poppy and Fred were avid divers, and she said knowing how to tie the bowline with your eyes closed and one hand behind your back might save a life.

We fumbled and laughed, and I never quite got the bowline right with one hand behind my back, but I practiced the regular way more and felt proficient enough. After wandering back into the cockpit, we refreshed our drinks and found Fred and Eivind in the main salon, Eivind strumming a guitar.

When I walked in, Eivind looked up at me and gave me a soft smile. He strummed quiet and low, chatting with Fred as his hands worked.

I took a moment to admire the sight—and of course, he caught me doing so—before I slipped back out into the cockpit.

Poppy, the perfect hostess, brought out nibbles and topped up drinks. My day in the sun was catching up to me, and I yawned with more and more frequency. Marcella asked if I wanted to join them for dinner, and I declined, opting to call the multitude of Poppy's cheese and crackers I'd eaten a meal.

I made my goodbyes, and Eivind appeared by my side.

"Let me walk you back home," he said, looping an arm over my shoulder. We ambled down the dock. "Did you have a good day today?"

"I did. I almost got sucked into another boat project with Peter, but Edith came to my rescue." I grinned at him sideways.

"Boat projects are not fun."

"Not fun at all. I've only done one, but it was oily." I wrinkled my nose. "And a little smelly. And *really* hot and sticky."

He laughed. "So, we cannot expect you to help with the bilge?"

"You'd have to make it worth my time."

"Oh really?" He raised an eyebrow.

I nodded and yawned yet again.

"The free-diving lessons wore you out," Eivind said.

"Yes, I think so. I'll sleep well tonight. Hey, did you hear on the radio about the open mic night tomorrow?"

"Yes, I did. That is what Fred and I were talking about."

"Are you going to borrow his guitar?"

Eivind chuckled. "Maybe. Or maybe I will play my ukulele. One way or another, do not worry." He leaned into my ear. "I will seduce you."

I blushed and we laughed together, walking up to *Silver Lining*. Peter and Edith were sitting in the cockpit and Eivind waved a hand in greeting.

"Thanks for walking me home," I said, grinning.

"You are welcome." Eivind's hands rested on my hips and gave a gentle squeeze. "I will see you tomorrow." He kissed my cheek and, with a nod to our audience, walked back the way we'd come.

I climbed on board and collapsed into the corner of the cockpit.

Edith chortled. "Looks like you've had a fun day, my dear. Tell us all about it!"

Nine

I OPENED THE DOORS OF THE RESTAURANT WHICH WAS packed for open mic night. Some of the long-term marina residents, many of whom I'd met, were already up on stage. Guitars were being tuned, and musical instruments had been stacked up against the wall: guitar cases and a saxophone stand. A woman stood nearby with a bagpipe.

I spotted the crew of *Eik* in the corner and waved, but I made my way to the bar first. I found one of the last free stools and sat before ordering my beer.

A throat cleared into the microphone, and Donny, a Scottish sailor two slips down from *Silver Lining* who'd been here nearly as long as Edith and Peter, stood at the mic, holding a guitar.

"Testing, testing . . . all right, everyone! Welcome to open mic night at the marina. We have a few new faces and instruments this week, and some of our regulars are here. If you want to take the next song, grab your instrument and come on up to the side here, and I'll turn it over when I'm done. We've got Randy here on drums, and there are a few miscellaneous instruments anyone can grab on the stand over here. So if you feel like shaking a tambourine, well, then by God come shake a tambourine. Now, I'm gonna start us off with a little classic Jimmy Buffett."

He strummed the guitar, playing the first bar of a song that sounded familiar, but I couldn't name it. I was too young to fully appreciate Jimmy Buffett, but Randy kicked in behind him, and Donny's wife, Rae, grabbed a shaker from the side of the stage.

I sipped my beer and watched as Donny played a few songs, warming the crowd up. Another cruiser took his place to play a few rounds of American country music. By now a few people were on the dance floor, an American couple I knew doing a two-step and a few others swaying to the music.

I exchanged greetings with the couple who sat down next to me, vaguely familiar, and when I turned back to the stage, my eyebrows rose. Eivind sat in the wings, waiting for the next song. He held a ukulele in one hand and a stool in the other.

After the final bars of a Garth Brooks song, the guitarist bowed and stepped down off the stage, letting Eivind take a turn.

"Hallo, everyone," he said into the microphone as he set the stool down. "I am Eivind, from *Eik*. My friends gave me this ukulele"—he held it up—"when I moved onto the boat, as a joke. But who is laughing now?" There were a few light chuckles in the audience as Eivind strummed and tuned. "I play guitar, but this is my first performance with this beauty, so be gentle." Eivind grinned, and I couldn't help but smile at him. His eyes found mine.

Suddenly his hand flew over the strings as he played a fast and furious rhythm. Just a few notes in, he started to sing; it was "I Wanna Be Your Man" by the Beatles.

Eivind's eyes left mine to look down at his fingers, and I could breathe again. His voice carried, grittier than the original, but the tone was the same, hopeful and desperate all at the same time.

We hooted and cheered for him as he smiled and strummed. Randy backed him up with a lot of cymbals, and the energy climbed palpably. Dancers spun to the upbeat tempo.

As the song finished, the audience broke into applause.

"Thank you," Eivind said. "There's no one up here yet, so I think you are stuck with me for another."

A loud cheer came up, especially from behind me, where the rest of the crew of *Eik* sat.

This time, Eivind plucked the melody out first, a few quick notes on the strings and a few chords, and he started into the lyrics of "Hello, I Love You" by the Doors.

For the next song, Eivind slowed down and the couples on the dance floor held each other close. Another guitarist stood by waiting, so Eivind wrapped up and took a bow, leaving the stage to rambunctious applause.

The next singer started out with more classics, James Taylor, I think. I finished my beer and turned to flag the bartender down when a body came up behind me.

"Dance with me."

Eivind stood close to me, his breath warm on my cheek. I turned and he reached out a hand, which I grabbed and used to hop off my barstool. Eivind weaved around tables and people to lead us out to the dance floor. It was crowded, dancers and conversation filling the room, but I only had eyes for Eivind. He glanced back once, and my stomach flipped. This was not the Eivind I was used to, the carefree, flirty Eivind.

This Eivind needed me.

He swapped hands with me behind his back and then pulled me in close. I put an arm over his shoulders and we swayed to the music. My nose came to Eivind's collarbone, and I closed my eyes and inhaled, savoring the way he smelled, his usual scent edged with something a little rougher: sweat and heat.

Eivind's sense of rhythm worked just as well on the dance floor as it did onstage. We swayed together, keeping our bodies close, our heartbeats matching.

The song wound down, and the singer spoke into the microphone. Eivind and I reluctantly broke apart and turned to the stage. "We have a special duet we're going to play tonight. You all know and love Greta's bagpipes, so we're going to strike it up with a classic."

The guitarist fingered a melody and the drums joined in with a strong and steady beat. When he shifted to strumming, Greta came in with her bagpipes. Everyone cheered and the crowd knew what to do.

"Oooh, what will we do with a drunken sailor?" the guitarist called into the mic. He pulled back and the audience responded.

"What will we do with a drunken sailor?"

The dance floor became a whirlwind. Eivind led, spinning me, and with everyone else we galloped around, laughing and carrying on like the drunken sailors we were.

I laughed when they sang the rest of the verses. Everyone knew the question, but the answer was more obscure: *put him in bed with the captain's daughter*, who was, apparently, not attractive.

Eivind and I spun around the dance floor with the masses. After the song finished, we moved back to the table with the rest of the *Eik* crew. One drink became more. Eivind ordered shots. I danced with Marcella and Elayna when a guitarist played some pop covers, and then Elayna struggled to drag Jonas onto the dance floor, only succeeding to coax him out for a slow song.

My hair escaped its confines, and Eivind couldn't stop touching it, his fingers twirling at the nape of my neck.

Time flew, and the musicians tired. Eventually the music switched to piped-in radio, and the atmosphere got quieter. We were closing down the place.

Ten

AS WE WALKED BACK TO THE BOATS, EIVIND AND I TRAILED behind the other three. I was delightfully buzzed and happy.

"I know this sounds insane," I said, "but I want to go into the jungle."

Eivind laughed, his arm around my neck and his fingers intertwined with mine. "Yes, insane. Why do you want to go into the jungle?"

"I want to see the darkness of it. Like, it's such a raw, natural place, and if you go in there, the darkness will just be . . ." I trailed off, not knowing how to finish my thought.

"Hmm . . ." Eivind kissed my forehead. "I'll take you into the dark."

"What? Really? Don't you think it'll be dangerous?"

"What is dangerous here? Anything we come across will hear and see us first. It will run. And we won't go deep. Stay here, okay? I will be right back."

"Okay. Right here." I pointed at the dock below my feet.

Eivind's eyes crinkled in amusement as he turned and retreated down the dock. I gazed up at the sky, looking for a few constellations I might know, everything so new to me here in the northern hemisphere.

Eivind was back quickly and he handed me a strap of some kind.

"Here, put this on."

I peered at it in the dark: it was a headlamp, the kind someone might wear for spelunking. Eivind pulled his headlamp on and I did the same. He reached over to click the button on mine, and his face lit up in a red glow.

"It's red so you can see better at night. Now, let's go find this darkness of yours."

Eivind looped his arm back around me and we walked out toward the road. "You use these headlamps on the boat?"

"Yes, we use red light most of the time, because your eyes do not have to adjust from red to dark. But they adjust from white to dark, right, and it is hard to see sometimes. This is better."

"That makes sense," I said.

"Did you not camp when you were a child?"

"We did, but we used white flashlights and were always camping in campgrounds and not out in the wilderness. Besides, you have to drive *far* from Sydney to find dark skies away from the lights of the city."

"You never went to the Outback?" Eivind asked.

It took me a moment to respond; my eyes were glued to my feet, making sure the headlamp lit up my path. "No, it was always too far away, too expensive. By the time maybe we could afford it, I was a teenager and too cool to want to go vacationing with my parents." I sighed and dramatically leaned my head against Eivind's shoulder. "Maybe someday. I bet you have some amazing dark nights at sea!"

"Yes, we do. Okay, stop here."

I looked around. We were far enough into the jungle that the foliage blocked the lights from the marina. Eivind took his headlamp off, and I took mine off too. We faced each other, and Eivind pointed the beam of his light right between us; my headlamp dangled from my hand. He grinned, looking wicked in the red light and shadows.

"Ready?"

"Ready!"

We both clicked our headlamps off at the same time. I could barely see a thing, the inky blackness of the jungle surrounding me. I reached a hand out into the darkness.

"Right here." Eivind stepped closer, and my palm rested on his chest. We stayed still as our eyes adjusted. There were sounds all around me: insects talking into the night, the occasional far-off call of a bird, Eivind's breathing and my own. I could barely make out the path stretching ahead and behind us, and the sky full of stars overhead was hidden by the giant leaves of the jungle, a negative space of shadows. Here, without the heat and noise of the crowds, I breathed more deeply, inhaling the woodsy smell.

Eivind took another step toward me and his hand came up to my waist. We were so close, and his thumb slipping between the waistband of my shorts and the hem of my T-shirt electrified me. I'd heard that when you were deprived of one of your senses, the others became heightened.

So what would it feel like to kiss Eivind in the dark?

His nose touched mine, his lips a breath away from my own.

"Don't kiss me," I whispered.

Eivind stopped and swallowed thickly. "Why not?"

"If we kiss, you'll kick me off the boat."

"What?" Eivind took a small step back.

"I mean . . ." Ugh. How could I explain it? The alcohol made my mind stutter. "I don't want to join the boat with some drama or baggage already. Like, this is the whole reason I came to Panama, and if this doesn't work out, I've risked a lot of money for nothing."

"It will not be drama." He smoothed some of my hair back behind my ears. "A kiss doesn't have to mean drama."

I poked his stomach, then let my hands linger. Distraction! "Come on, Eivind. You know sleeping together always comes with some form of drama or another."

"Sleeping together? I thought we were just kissing," he teased as he grabbed my hand.

I felt myself blush, invisible in the darkness, and pulled my hand away. "You know what I mean."

"Yes, I know. And you are right: we do not really need more drama."

"Wait, what? *More* drama?"

"Oh." Eivind winced. "Well . . . Jonas and Elayna . . . sometimes . . ."

"Mm-hmm. See, more drama!" I poked his stomach again and controlled myself enough this time not to feel him up.

He laughed. "All right, all right, I will not kiss you."

"Thank you."

"That may be the first time I have ever been thanked for *not* kissing." He tugged me to his side and pointed us back in the direction of the marina. "Now, let's take this non-kissing girl to bed so she can sleep!"

Eleven

THE NEXT MORNING, I WAS NESTLED INTO MY CABIN ON *Silver Lining* when a voice that didn't belong to Edith or Peter came from the salon. Propped up with pillows, I sat reclined against the slanted wall of my cabin, reading. A few moments passed before someone knocked on my door.

"Come in," I called.

The door opened, and Eivind's head poked into my cabin. "Hallo." He grinned at me.

"Hey," I said. "Welcome to my humble abode." I gestured my arms wide to take in the room.

Eivind chuckled, stepped in, and closed the door behind him. He sat on the edge of my bed and swung his bare feet up so he sat across from me, leaning on the other side. I grabbed another pillow and tossed it to him.

97

"Thank you." He supported his back and rested his hand on my feet, which were crossed at the ankles. Eivind's legs were too long, and he had to bend his knees, pressing his toes into the wall next to me.

"What's up on *Eik* today?"

Eivind stroked my anklebone with his thumb. "We are joining the morning group for a walk in the jungle. Come with us?"

"Sounds great. I've been meaning to do that, but Edith likes her mornings slow and she's been a bad influence." I checked my watch. We had fifteen minutes to get to the meeting point.

I put my e-reader aside and nudged Eivind's feet. He pulled his legs up so I could climb out of my bunk and sort through my clothing options. I wore gym shorts and a loose tank top with no bra, but I had a clean sports bra and a T-shirt to change into. I dug for a little while, looking for a clean pair of socks. Living on the boat meant I was constantly running around barefoot or in thongs; my socks had migrated down to the bottom of my bag.

When I turned around, Eivind had slid down, lying on his back in my bed with his legs up against the wall.

"I have to change."

Eivind turned his head to face the corner. "I will not look."

I peeked around and his eyes were closed too. Just to be sure, I grabbed one of the pillows and put it on his head. He chuckled and pressed the pillow into his face.

Swiftly, I stripped my top off and changed. When I was done, I patted Eivind's stomach and he jolted, the muscles flexing under my hand. He let out what sounded like a swear word in Norwegian and then raised the pillow to look at me.

I grinned. "Did I startle you?" I started to pull my hand away, but Eivind grabbed it, pressing my palm to his shirt. He gripped my arm with his other hand and pulled me, flipping me over his body to lie on his other side.

"What are you doing? I'm ready—let's go find your crew." I poked his side.

He twitched but closed his eyes for a moment, trying to relax on my bed. "This bed is rock hard. How are you sleeping here? Is this mattress concrete?" Then he opened his eyes and started pulling at the sheets, trying to investigate.

I reached over and swatted his hands away from the bedding. "Hush. It's free. And I like Edith and Peter. I think they usually use this room for storage, and they were nice enough to clean it out for me. I doubt they know how bad the bed is."

"You could always come to sleep in my bed," he teased.

"Nice try," I said.

He reached over and wrapped his arms around me. "My bed is much more comfortable. And I have been told I am excellent at cuddling."

"Mmm. I believe that." I snuggled into his side.

We were quiet for a few moments.

"So, you will come to sleep on our boat?"

I raised my head to look up at him. His heart beat strong under my palm, his warmth radiating through the fabric of his T-shirt. Eivind's eyes traveled down my face, coming to a stop on my lips. His eyelids grew heavy, his thumb coming up to trace my bottom lip.

Reaching over, I smooshed his cheeks together with my hand. "This is why I won't sleep in the same bed as you. No kissing."

"Whoops," Eivind said. The muscles in his cheeks pulled under my hand. "I pwomise. No kwissing."

He opened and closed his lips, puckering them up to make fish faces at me. I shook his head for him.

"Repeat after me. 'I, Eivind, solemnly swear.'"

He repeated after me, his *l*'s disappearing into a jumbled mess. *Sowomwy.* I laughed.

"'To not kiss Lila.'"

"Nowpe," Eivind said. He shook my hands off his face. "I think you should promise to me."

"I should promise to not kiss you?"

"No," he said, eyes mischievous. "I know you are tempted right now, but repeat after me." He grabbed my face with his hand and made me a fish face this time. I giggled. "'I, Lila, solemnly swear.'"

I rolled my eyes and repeated after him as best I could.

"'To kiss Eivind.'"

I protested, but he held up a finger.

"Wait, wait, wait. 'To kiss Eivind,'" he reiterated.

I gave him a look. He shook my head gently.

"'To kiss Eivind.'" I mumbled the words, and he grinned.

"On our last night together." His grin faded as he watched me.

I cocked my head at him, and he released my face.

"Promise me," he whispered.

"I, Lila, solemnly swear to kiss you on our last night together." My voice was husky.

"Okay." Eivind reared back, putting some space between us. "Now, I promise, I will not try to kiss you again. You get to kiss me. I can wait."

I laughed and pressed my face into his chest, attempting to hide a very pleased smile. Eivind was one of the sweetest guys I'd ever met.

"Lila! Eivind!" Edith called us through the door. "Jonas is waiting outside."

Reluctantly, Eivind and I rolled out of bed and went to join Jonas, Marcella, and Elayna on the dock. Edith sent me off with a bottle of water, which I slipped into Eivind's backpack while he pulled on his trainers.

We mingled with the group of walkers in front of the hotel and introduced ourselves to the leader, Francois, who I had talked to on the radio but hadn't met yet, and at the designated time we took off into the woods. We followed a thick trail with lush jungle on either side. A few minutes into the walk we had to clear the path for a car, so technically, it must have been a road. Several walkers had binoculars. We weren't a quiet bunch, conversing with one another. But we still managed to spot so many interesting critters.

At one point Francois stopped us and pointed into the trees. He grinned at me as I stood beside him, peering into the jungle.

Several trees over, branches started to sway. The thick foliage blocked my view. I craned my neck, standing on my tippy-toes, as if that would help.

I heard it: the same call I heard every day. It reverberated through the forest, echoing off the trees. A flash of black fur peeked through the leaves.

Suddenly, from behind me, another call sounded. It echoed from further away, so I didn't bother looking for it, but the monkeys were communicating across the jungle—and we were in the middle.

"Uh, should we be worried?" I whisper-hissed to Francois.

"No, you are perfectly safe."

Just to be sure, I inched a little closer to Eivind and froze, looking up into the trees, catching glimpses of the animals here and there.

Finally one cleared the leaves. Following closely behind, six or so more came into view, some smaller than the others. I watched them climb in the canopy, wrapping their hands, feet, and tails around branches and vines.

One monkey paused, hanging upside down from two vines. His legs were spread-eagle from vine to vine, proudly showing off his goods to anyone who cared to look. His tail tightly gripped one of the vines.

Rotating his head, he watched us, watched the jungle, watched his fellow monkeys. Still dangling, he howled—not necessarily at us, but perhaps at the jungle around him and to anyone who would listen.

The group around me chuckled as he howled again and bounced up and down, giving us a floppy X-rated show. Perhaps disappointed in our response, he moved on.

The group of monkeys passed overhead, climbing out onto the branches of the trees on one side of the road and leaping across to the other side.

I took this all in, reeling in the knowledge that I stood in a completely different world than I'd ever known. Close encounters of the jungle kind were an unexpected benefit of this trip so far. In all my planning, I'd never imagined being someplace so wild.

Twelve

WHEN THE MONKEYS MOVED ALONG, WE DID TOO. I couldn't take my eyes off the canopy, hoping that more monkeys would approach. But we'd left them behind.

The walking group didn't last very long. Jonas had struck up a conversation with one of the men, and they talked about an old military base further into the jungle.

"What do you think, Lila? Should we go explore the base?" Jonas asked.

"I'm in," I said, and Eivind pumped his fist.

The crew of *Eik* and I separated from the group, waved goodbye, and walked deeper into the jungle.

We came upon a huge vine hanging from the canopy into the path. It was thicker than my wrist and barely had any leaves.

Eivind grabbed the vine and tested its strength. He looked at his brother, who grinned at him.

Launching himself as high as he could, Eivind grabbed the vine and pulled himself up. His feet wrapped around it, knees clamped together. With a few heaves, his feet were up over my head.

Oh dear God, please don't let this vine break.

Eivind stopped and bounced on the vine a little bit. He climbed a few meters more and carefully slid down. When his feet were on the ground, he said something in Norwegian to Jonas.

Grabbing the vine, Jonas pulled himself up the same way his brother had, muscles straining as he rose hand over hand. He stopped and said something to Eivind, who laughed but never took his eyes off Jonas.

"What did he say?" I asked.

"I told him getting down was the harder part and not to go too high. Jonas basically said, 'Oops.'"

Jonas fumbled a little bit getting his feet to slip through the vine as he descended. When he stood on safe ground again, Eivind pulled his shirt off and wiped the sweat from his face. Tucking the shirt into the back of his shorts, he faced me.

"Your turn."

"Wait, what?" I squealed as Eivind grabbed my hips from behind and lifted me up. I gripped the vine and Eivind tried to release me gently.

"Hold on to the vine," he said.

"I am!"

He chuckled as he lowered me down until his hands left my hips and I dangled off the vine. I lasted two seconds before I dropped off and Eivind caught me.

"How do you even do that? I don't know what to do."

Eivind held me up while he showed me how to tangle my feet in the vine. It was tough; the vine was thick and didn't flex much under my feet. But once I had my feet right, I grabbed the vine again with my hands.

Eivind let go and took a step back.

"Ah!" I shouted into the jungle. "I'm doing it!"

Eivind chuckled and encouraged me to try to climb up. I leaned back and looked at him upside down, standing with his arms out, waiting to catch me if I fell.

"Nah, I'm good."

He grinned. "You are good there? Just hanging out?"

I giggled. "Push me."

Eivind laughed and grabbed my hips, pulling me back and then letting go. I swung out toward Elayna, who caught me and, laughing, pushed me back to Eivind.

I went back and forth a few times, but then I had to call it quits, so Eivind helped me down. My legs shook, the insides of my thighs sore from holding on so tight with my feet.

Elayna and Marcella took turns, and I watched, impressed by Elayna's upper body strength. While she didn't climb anywhere near as high as Jonas and Eivind, she managed to climb a few strides up the vine.

They took turns swinging, the rest of us pushing them around our group. I absentmindedly fended them off, but my eyes kept drawing back to Eivind. His biceps were swollen and sweaty and flushed . . .

He caught me looking at him and winked. I blushed and kept my eyes to myself until everyone had taken their turn swinging and we moved on.

It didn't take long to find the ruins—what used to be Fort Sherman, an American military base built over a hundred years ago.

It had been abandoned for a long time, and the jungle was reclaiming the land. The five of us wandered through the base, tramping down on leaves and empty shell casings all over the ground. Everyone had brought headlamps except for me. Eivind grabbed my hand and pulled me to explore with him.

Up and down we went, trodding stone staircases to the roofs and exploring dark passages. We found jail cells for prisoners and a chapel for the faithful. In tunnels that reeked of guano, bats flew past in the darkness.

Mortar bases were strategically located in some of the buildings, their barrels gone, but identifiable by their large round embrasures.

Eivind stood behind one and brought his fists up, guiding an invisible weapon. He mimicked the sounds of gunfire, his arms shaking from his imaginary rapid-fire weapon.

He peered as though looking through a scope. "What do you suppose they were fighting anyway?"

"I think it was a training base. The US was training its men in jungle warfare."

He grunted. "That was certainly not something I trained for in Norway."

"What? You were in the military?"

"Do not sound so surprised. In Norway, everyone must apply. I do not know the word in English."

"Conscription?"

"Is that what it is?"

"Yes." I nodded. "Conscription. I can't picture you in the military."

Eivind straightened up and stepped closer. He cocked his head at me. "Why?"

"I guess I think of military men like our ANZAC veterans. Gruff and hard. Older."

Eivind's voice dropped. "You don't think I'm hard?" He took a step closer and I backed up.

"Well, no, of course I think you're hard. I mean, not *hard* hard, but tough."

Eivind took another step forward, and I backed up more, hitting the wall. He brought his arms up on either side of my head. Then I made the mistake of putting my hands on his biceps.

"Definitely hard," I squeaked.

Eivind leaned in and pressed a kiss just beneath my ear. He inhaled deeply before taking a step back. "Everyone must apply, but no one serves unless they want to. I served because Jonas had done his service too. He said it was our duty."

I rebuilt myself from the puddle of Lila on the ground and nodded. Quieter, darker Jonas would be serious about military service.

Eivind gestured onward, grabbing my hand, and we emerged from the bunker to find the rest of the crew seated on a grassy patch, snacking. I dragged Eivind to join them and Marcella gave me a biscuit from her plastic bin—she had well over a dozen chocolate chip oatmeal biscuits. I tried to pull my hand back, but Eivind ignored me and I ate with one hand.

The longer we sat in silence, the more noises the jungle made. I leaned against Eivind and closed my eyes, listening to the whistles and rustles around us and Eivind devouring cookies. It reminded me of a white noise machine, and I relaxed against him.

Before I could pass out, Eivind nudged me, and we all dusted ourselves off to head back home. I returned to *Silver Lining* for dinner, and spent the next day, my last with Edith and Peter before moving aboard *Eik*, hung over.

Thirteen

I WAS, QUITE POSSIBLY, VIBRATING FROM EXCITEMENT. Today was the day. I was moving on board *Eik*, and we were starting our transit of the Panama Canal. I put up a post on Facebook with a link to the webcams and our approximate transit time, and I sent the same information to my parents via email, plus I had a conversation with my mum before packing up my stuff on *Silver Lining*. I gave Peter and Edith a few gifts: some of Edith's favorite chocolates to replenish the supply I'd been dipping into and a collection of random candy bars.

We tearfully hugged goodbye, and I promised to email them updates. Edith said cruising friendships are like jack-in-the-boxes: you never knew when they would pop up again. I hoped she was right.

I'd walked the docks with my stubby last night, saying goodbye to everyone who'd ever invited me on board for a drink or dinner, anyone who'd performed at open mic night or played dominoes with me. Many of them gave me boat cards—business cards, but with the name of their boat and their contact info—and told me to keep in touch.

I had flopped onto my bed afterward and cried a little. I'd become attached to these people, this place, this lifestyle. I thought about how cruisers like Peter and Edith were always on the move, finding tight-knit groups like this one and then moving on. How could they keep that up?

It helped that they had each other. Peter and Edith were my life goals: the idea that you could have someone you were willing to live with in a small space for years, making fast but fleeting friendships as you went.

This cruising lifestyle was such a juxtaposition of fast friendships and quick goodbyes.

I heaved my backpacks on, grabbed a few bags of miscellaneous stuff to bring over, and made my way to *Eik*. The crew welcomed me aboard, and I threw my backpacks in the new cabin I was to share with Marcella.

When I emerged, the rest of the crew waited, sitting around the table. I slid into the booth next to Marcella, and Jonas brought me up to speed.

"Robert said we need to be at the anchorage at three o'clock, so we will leave here at two to give ourselves plenty of time. The advisor"—the person who would ride through the canal for the day with us—"will board at three thirty. We are going through side-tied to a bigger boat, so it's very little work for us. We will still have to be careful attaching and detaching, and I will still have all of you set up on a different quarter of the boat to help me out."

I was a little disappointed not to be needed, but more than anything, I felt relieved to have less pressure on me to do the lines right.

Jonas continued. "Marcella will be responsible for dinner tonight, and Elayna will help her. That way Eivind and I can focus on tying the boat up to the mooring ball in the lake and we will not have dinner too late.

"Any questions?"

We all shook our heads.

"Then, in thirty-six hours, we will be partying in the Pacific Ocean!" Jonas was happier than I'd ever seen him. I was sure he was nervous, too, but he didn't show it.

We split up to get some chores done. Marcella worked in the kitchen, putting dishes away. Eivind signaled for me and we went up on deck together. The day before, Robert had delivered some supplies to the boat: long lines and these round, comically huge things Eivind said were fenders. Instead of the white cylindrical inflatables most boats at the dock had, these were bright orange.

Eivind showed me how to tie one to the lifelines, and we practiced over and over again. He explained that the fenders would go between the boats to protect them from each other. One of my jobs would be to adjust the height to make sure the boats didn't cause damage as they knocked together.

The rest of the crew joined us on the deck. Jonas started the engine, which came to life growling and vibrating under my feet. Marcella and Elayna were on the dock, and Jonas barely gave them instructions. Everyone had a job and they knew exactly what to do. Elayna stepped on board with one line in her hand, so now it was only Marcella on the dock, with one last line tying the boat to it. Marcella took it off the cleat, threw it over the lifelines, and *Eik* started to move backward out of the slip. Marcella hustled down the dock to the gate and climbed on board.

Eik swung wide out into the water, and Jonas shifted the engine into forward gear. The boat picked up speed, making the tight turns around the dock and then out the entrance of the marina. The whole time the rest of the crew had their places, calling out information to Jonas, who adjusted accordingly.

"Three meters off the stern!"

"The edge of the dock is right here."

"Whoa, check out the crocodile onshore!"

We all looked starboard to find the beast sunbathing on the sandbank. I shuddered.

Once clear of the entrance, the crew coiled up the dock lines and piled them by the mast. The giant orange fenders went over the sides, and they bounced against the hull with each swell.

Out ahead of us, Colón loomed with a bit of a haze around the city. Behind us, past the break wall, were dozens of ships waiting in the ocean.

I walked back toward Jonas and sat down behind him and to the right, in the corner of the bench. I could see all the instruments and gadgets he watched, and Jonas spun the wheel to adjust course.

He reached down to click a button labeled AUTO and took his hands off the steering wheel. It continued to move without him, and a gentle whirring continued beneath our feet.

"Want to see the chart?" He pointed to the screen.

"Sure." I sat up to look at it.

The display showed a map in orange and blue, and Jonas explained where we were: a small boat icon in the middle of the screen. He touched some buttons and the view zoomed out. There were a whole bunch of shapes—rectangles with a point on one end—out beyond the coast.

"What are those?"

"This is our AIS—automatic identification system. All big ships have it, and most bigger sailboats do too. It broadcasts information about your boat—location and course—to other boats. These icons are all the big ships out at anchor."

He zoomed out further. There weren't dozens of ships . . . there were at least a hundred!

"What are they all doing?"

"They are waiting for their turn in the canal. Just like we will be."

"Wow. That's amazing."

"It costs time and money to go around South America, so unless the ship is too big, it will be going through here."

"How big is too big?"

Jonas shook his head. "They build ships specifically to fit in the Panama Canal. I do not remember how big.

Hundreds of meters, maybe." Jonas pulled back on the throttle and shouted at the rest of the crew on deck. "Time to anchor!"

We approached the rear of a small cluster of sailboats. Eivind gave Jonas the okay and walked to the bow of the boat. Elayna came to the gate at the lifelines and watched Jonas.

Jonas carefully steered the boat to approach the back of the catamaran *Starry Horizons*, which had been at the marina too. I'd met the owners, David and Amy, a young American couple, while walking the docks with Edith.

Eivind and Jonas worked together to drop our anchor. When we were set, the brothers gave each other another okay, and Jonas shut off the engine.

"Wow, you make it look easy."

Jonas smiled. "Lots of practice."

The crew all came back to the cockpit, and we settled in to wait. It was 2:20, and Jonas said he expected the advisor to be late.

"Lila," Elayna said, "I understand you have been playing dominoes at the marina. Would you teach us?"

Fourteen

I TAUGHT THEM HOW TO PLAY MEXICAN TRAIN DOMINOES.
Jonas played but stayed near the radio. He talked to the
other boats waiting, who confirmed they had not heard
from the canal yet.

Finally a call came for one of the other boats. We
listened in as they were told the pilot boat was en route
to their location with the advisor on board. We watched
as the pilot boat came up to the sailboat and an advisor
hopped onto the deck.

The pilot boat came our way, so Jonas opened the
gate. The advisor stepped on board. Jonas shook hands
with him, and they retreated to the cockpit where the
rest of us sat.

The advisor introduced himself and shook our
hands. "I am Manny," he said. "We're going to have a
great passage today, yes?"

"Yeah!" Eivind threw out a fist, and we all chuckled.

"It's easy, so easy today. I know the guys on the tugboat—they are a great crew. We will make sure that everyone is safe, yes? We will take good care of the boat." He clapped Jonas on the shoulder, and Jonas smiled nervously.

"Let's go talk about your setup." Manny and Jonas walked out onto the deck of the boat. The rest of us trailed behind. "This side you will tie up to the tugboat. You need three lines: bow, stern, and spring." Elayna walked over to where the dock lines had been stored when we left the marina and picked out three lines.

"Who will be on this side?" Manny asked Jonas.

"Eivind and Elayna," Jonas said, pointing.

"You two will pass the looped end over to the tugboat, and when the crew of the tug has secured the lines, then you cleat off on your side. Okay?"

Eivind and Elayna nodded.

"When you are done, come over here." Manny led us to the other side of the boat. "You will fend off the next sailboat on this side. You two"—he pointed to me and Marcella—"you will catch the lines from the other sailboat and put them on your cleats. Yes?"

I nodded, but glanced at Eivind. He smiled encouragingly.

Manny clapped Jonas on the shoulder again. "The sailboat next to you will take care of themselves. Any questions?" We shook our heads.

With a radio clipped onto his shoulder, he called the canal and told them we were ready. "It will be a little while," he said apologetically. "Let's wait in the shade."

We were going to be doing a lot of waiting.

Jonas and Manny talked strategy a bit, and Eivind listened in. Manny's radio went off occasionally, and he'd listen to the Spanish chatter and then return to our conversation, picking right back up where he'd left off. I fidgeted with the hem of my shorts. Opened my book. Put it down. Walked the length of the boat to the bow, looking at the anchor chain angling down into the sludge of the harbor.

Eivind came up to join me. "You okay?" he asked quietly.

"Manny said we put the lines around the cleat. Can we practice that again?"

Eivind chuckled. "Actually, the boat will pass you a loop, just like we will pass to the tugboat. So you just have to feed the line under the lifelines and put the loop around the cleat. It is really easy."

"Oh." My shoulders slumped in relief. "That is easy. Okay."

"Plus, once my line is done, I will come over and help you."

Manny called out from the cockpit. "That's the big ship going in with you."

A cargo ship came in from the ocean. One tugboat was in front of it and another behind.

Nervousness forgotten, I gasped. "Oh my God. It's finally happening!" I grabbed Eivind's arm and shook it. He laughed. We watched the ship pass by, listening to the engines of the tugboats and watching the army of crew on the decks going about their jobs.

Jonas called out to us. "Time to go!"

Fifteen

EIVIND TOOK OFF FOR THE BOW AGAIN, AND I WENT WITH him to watch him work. When Jonas gave the signal, Eivind grabbed a remote from the locker underneath us. He pressed a button, and the chain started to retract into the boat. The clacking was the links of the chain hitting the crank.

Jonas and Eivind raised the anchor, and we motored toward the canal.

I stayed out of the way while the big fenders were moved to the port side of the boat. Soon we approached the huge concrete gates and entered the first lock that would lift us up. We got to our stations, with me in the starboard stern, close to Jonas. Eivind waited across from me, on the port side.

My heart pounded as Eivind and then Elayna threw the lines to the tugboat. Then Eivind pulled on his line, wrestling *Eik* closer. He strained, biceps bulging and causing my heart to stutter.

"Eivind!" Jonas called. "Cleat off!"

Eivind wrapped the line around the cleat and secured it. He walked forward to where Elayna was still pulling her line in.

"Gently," Manny said to Jonas.

Together, Elayna and Eivind pulled *Eik* into place and tied her off. Jonas and Manny walked the side, checking fenders and lines before Manny radioed in for the next boat.

Eivind joined me, and we watched *Starry Horizons* enter the canal. The boat approached us from behind, pulling up close.

It wasn't so much a throw as a pass. Amy swung the line toward me while the boats were less than a meter apart. I pulled the loop outside the lifelines and hooked it onto the cleat. Amy took up the slack and pulled it tight. The boat slid toward us sideways, gently nudging *Eik*.

David and Jonas shook hands and grinned. They walked the length of the boats together, both checking the lines and fenders, making adjustments as needed. When they gave the okay, the advisors for each boat radioed in.

I had met David and Amy, but not the rest of their crew, who, like me, had flown in to participate in the canal. We made introductions all around, shaking hands over the rails of our two boats.

The advisors of the two boats talked together, the radio crackling between them. "Okay, guys, the gate is closing."

Both crews slipped to the back of their boats to watch the gate close. It moved quietly; if Manny hadn't said anything, I might not have noticed.

We all waited, fidgeting on the decks. I glanced down to where the water swirled beneath us, and pointed. "Look!"

"We are up two feet already," Manny said.

"What, really? It's so quiet."

The water continued to swirl and formed a little whirlpool behind us. I kept my eyes on the measurement marks on the side of the wall, and sure enough, the water level rose.

"This is so cool," I said. I may have been geeking out a little, but everyone else around me grinned too, even Jonas.

A squawk on the radio signaled the lifting was done. We waited for more movement. Finally the engine of the big ship in front of us throttled up, and a storm of backwash kicked out from under its stern.

Eik and *Starry Horizons* swayed backward as far as their lines would let them. Both crews scrambled to their positions, checking lines and fenders. With *Starry Horizons* being pushed back, my line was slack.

The advisor on the catamaran gave David instructions while Manny did the same for us.

"The catamaran is going to detach from us and fall back. When they are clear, we will detach from the tugboat, and fall back as well. The tug unties and goes forward out of the lock. We will follow him into the next lock and do the same thing we just did. Okay?"

We nodded and reported to our stations. Amy untied her line, giving me some slack to take it off the cleat.

"See you soon!" she called, laughing as they motored backward.

When we were loose from the tugboat, we backed up too. I watched David pivot his boat away from us, giving Jonas more room.

"Fucking catamarans." Eivind smirked.

"What does that mean?"

"They have two engines. They can turn on a dime. He's just showing off now." Eivind winked at me.

When the tug was clear, we motored through to the next lock and tied up. This time Amy was at the bow, so one of the guys tossed the line to me instead. He missed, and the loop splashed into the water.

"Hurry!" David called out from the helm. His friend pulled the line up and heaved it at me again. This time the toss was good, but I got slapped with wet rope. Eivind chuckled next to me and, once I got the loop on, I wiped my face off on his sleeve.

He grunted and laughed, pushing me away.

We sat together at the stern this time, dangling our legs over the back of the boat and watching the gates close. The water swirled again. We raised, detached, and did the whole thing one last time before motoring through into Gatun Lake.

We cheered and high-fived, but Jonas looked grim.

"Marcella, get started on dinner. Elayna, help with the lines."

I stood with Eivind. "

What's going on?" I asked him.

He grimaced. "We have to tie up to the mooring ball." He pointed to a large disk floating in the water with a metal loop on top. "It's not a regular mooring ball, and we have to share it." He shook his head. "This is going to be complicated."

I stayed out of the way as best I could. Eivind ended up jumping onto the mooring ball, which was big enough for him to lie down on. He ran lines from the bow and stern to the loop at the top, and when *Starry Horizons* came up to the other side of the mooring ball, we passed lines from bow to bow and stern to stern. A web of lines secured us all together.

Marcella had been busy cooking a Thai green curry dish, which Elayna bowled up and brought into the cockpit. We all—Manny included—ate quickly and quietly.

It was nearly seven o'clock. Jonas's eyes were lined with exhaustion and there was a slump to his shoulders. Eivind watched him carefully.

Elayna brought up a bottle of sparkling wine. "A toast!" she called out, popping the cork.

Eivind narrowed his eyes at her but accepted a glass. Raising it up, he said, "To Jonas. Great job getting us through today."

They hugged and slapped backs, and we downed our wine—all except Manny, who couldn't accept a drink on duty. Shortly after, his pilot boat came and Jonas walked him out to the gate and shook his hand. We all shouted and waved goodbye from the cockpit.

Eivind started rounding up empty glasses and dishes. "Okay, time to clean up and go to bed. It is an early morning tomorrow."

I grabbed a stack and followed Eivind behind, while Elayna whined, "It is barely eight. We have plenty of time."

Eivind ignored her and set Marcella to washing dishes while he cleaned the table in the cockpit. I dried the dishes and chatted with Marcella and we all tried to ignore Elayna's sulking.

Jonas had disappeared into his cabin, and he returned with a pillow and sheet. He passed Eivind and squeezed his shoulder before heading up to the cockpit. Eivind's eyes followed Jonas, worry creasing them.

Sixteen

THE NEXT MORNING I WOKE UP EARLY, BEFORE EVERYONE else. I crept out of my bunk quietly so as not to disturb Marcella, and poked my head out of the companionway. I spotted Jonas sleeping on the bench seat of the cockpit. A softly lit sky greeted me, and the sun peeked over the edge of the horizon.

A weight on the stairs settled behind me and a hand came into view on either side of me. Eivind gripped the handrail, and the warmth of his front pressed into my back through my clothes.

He whispered into my ear, "God morgen."

I turned my head a little and smiled at him. Eivind's warm breath brushed my face, minty fresh. He let his nose tickle my cheek just in front of my ear.

"Is Jonas okay?" I whispered.

Eivind looked at his brother and sighed. He rested his chin on my shoulder. "My brother is a good captain, but anyone would have been stressed yesterday. And he worried about this mooring. It is not comfortable. Hopefully, he slept enough out here, but I doubt it."

"Should we start making breakfast, or will that wake him up?"

"Mmm . . . I think not yet." Eivind brought an arm around my waist, pressing our bodies closer together. We stood for a few moments, cuddling in the doorway of *Eik*.

Eivind was an award-winning snuggler, even standing up. On the stairs, I stood a little bit taller than him, and he could perfectly nuzzle the curve of my neck. I leaned back and tilted my head. Eivind took the invitation and pressed a soft kiss into my neck that sent butterflies fluttering in my belly.

And then he nipped my neck. I moaned. He inhaled sharply and we pressed into each other more, and his hardness pushed against me—

"Eivind, what are you—" Marcella called from below. "Oh shit! Sorry!"

Out of the corner of my eye, Jonas stirred and blinked awake.

Eivind huffed a breath of laughter and squeezed me close one more time before letting go.

"Time to make some breakfast."

———

WE MOTORED THROUGH A RIVER OF CHOCOLATE MILK. Our new advisor, Diego, had come on board *Eik* after breakfast, and we had untied from the mooring and departed. We had several hours of motoring through Gatun Lake ahead of us before we would arrive at the second set of locks. Marcella and I played card games while Eivind drove the boat. He'd shooed Jonas down for a short nap while there was still time.

Diego was a quiet man, a contrast from the sociable Manny. He spent most of his time doing paperwork in the cockpit. After an hour or so Jonas came back up and took over again. Eivind sat down next to me, holding a book, his other arm behind me and his fingers absentmindedly stroking my shoulder.

Marcella and I had finished our game—I won—and I leaned back and tucked myself into Eivind's side.

"Whatcha reading?" I tapped the open page of his book.

"I am trying to improve my English." He showed me the cover—a young adult novel.

I looked up at him. "Your English is excellent."

"Thank you." He hugged my neck a little harder. "I feel comfortable talking, but I would like to read and write better. Have you read this one?"

I shook my head. "I enjoy young adult, but I prefer to read romance."

"Mmm." Eivind winked at me.

I smiled and let him go back to reading. I closed my eyes and drifted for a few minutes, listening to the hum of the engine and the sound of *Eik*'s wake.

I did have something I needed to do—book a hostel for the night. I grabbed my phone and pulled up some booking sites.

"Jonas, where exactly will you be dropping me off tonight?"

"Tonight?"

"Yeah, so I can book a bed."

Jonas looked at Eivind, who listened closely. "Lila, stay here tonight. Stay as long as you want. You can save yourself some money."

I looked at Eivind. "Are you okay with that?"

He squeezed me a bit closer. "Of course. We like you."

"Thank you." I kissed his cheek. "I appreciate it."

"Besides," he said. "You made me a promise . . ."

I snuggled back into Eivind, the flutters of anticipation tickling my belly.

Finally we approached the second set of locks. *Starry Horizons* waited, but the other boats coming through had not caught up to us. Jonas kept the boat drifting near the entrance, occasionally moving us upstream again and letting us float back down.

The small cruise ship we were waiting for arrived. It was five stories tall and a few hundred feet long, a miniature version of the cruise ships I had seen before. The ship entered the lock and tied up. When our advisor gave us the go-ahead, we motored up and tied on. *Starry Horizons* followed us and we were all secure.

However, our big ship hadn't arrived yet. It was going to come in behind us, so we waited. We resumed playing games, reading, chatting with our neighbors, whatever we could do to occupy our time. Some of the cruise ship passengers leaned over the rail and struck up a conversation with us.

I glanced over my shoulder; our bigger lock companion had arrived, a massive cruise ship approaching from behind. There wasn't much room on this side of the canal, and I suspected the other side also had a narrow gap. The Panama Canal mules lined up: small locomotives that ran on a track and hauled the big ships forward. They were named mules because, before the rail existed, actual mules pulled the ships around. The bow came closer and closer until it finally towered over us and I had to crane my neck to take it all in.

A few minutes later the gates were closed and the water started to drain. We dropped ten meters in the first step down from Gatun Lake to join the Pacific Ocean. The rest of the locks went smoothly, repeating the same motion twice more. In the second lock, a behemoth of a ship passed us on the other side of the lock, headed to Gatun Lake. The advisor told us they called the ship a RORO—Roll-On, Roll-Off—and it transported vehicles like cars. It made the cruise ship behind us look small.

We reached the last lock. It took even longer than the others. Eivind and I perched on the bow of *Eik* as the water drop down the gauge. When it stopped dropping, we waited.

And waited.

I swung my legs in circles underneath me, kicking my bare feet out and bumping Eivind's with every circle. When I annoyed him enough, he pinched my bare thigh, and I squealed and squirmed away before slinking back to knock him again.

"Look!" Jonas called out.

Like curtains being pulled away, the last gate opened to reveal a massive bridge and the Pacific Ocean. The sailors on both boats whooped and hollered. One of the crew members on *Starry Horizons* blew a conch horn, low and triumphant.

We'd made it through the Panama Canal!

Seventeen

W<small>E MOTORED OUT, PASSING UNDER THE</small> B<small>RIDGE OF</small> the Americas—the suspension bridge connecting North America to South America—and we floated in the river while Diego departed on a pilot boat. We stopped one more time for Robert to collect the fenders and dock lines, and then we pulled into Panama City near the delta and picked up a mooring ball at La Playita Marina.

The rest of the crew had a few things to do: lines were washed, coiled, and left on the lifelines to dry. Marcella walked around the deck with a bucket of water, scrubbing away dirt with a wet brush. Elayna cleaned all the dishes from the day. Jonas wrote his captain's log and Eivind dropped the dinghy into the water, the small inflatable boat kept on the stern of *Eik* that would take us to shore now that we were away from a dock.

We each disappeared into our rooms or the heads, getting ready for a night out to celebrate. I dressed in the nicest clothes I had, a pair of jean shorts and a flowing camisole. I even put on mascara and a bit of lip stain Elayna had shared. It had been weeks since I'd put on makeup.

I stepped out of my cabin the same time Eivind stepped out of his.

He looked me up and down appreciatively, while I did the same with him. He was dressed in a polo shirt, shorts, and boat shoes. One might have called it Euro prep, but that was how cruisers dressed up—their normal outfit without the threadbare holes.

"Lila," he said breathlessly, "you look beautiful." A finger came up and traced my exposed collarbone. I loved how much Eivind touched me, but it had been turning me on ever since I'd moved aboard. And now, knowing we were finished with our trip through the canal and I could stay here or leave for a hostel whenever I wanted.

As if Eivind could read my thoughts, he stared at me intensely, and his eyes held the possibility of everything we could do tonight.

I almost kissed him. But he beat me to it, bringing his lips to my shoulder, where his finger had just been.

The kiss was wet and soft, and he followed it with more, trailing up my neck. I gasped, gripping his shirt in my fists and pressing myself against him.

"I love your neck," he murmured against my skin.

A weak laugh escaped my lips. "I can tell."

Eivind inched us back against the wall, his hands sliding down my body to cup my butt.

"LILA! EIVIND! DO NOT GET DISTRACTED DOWN THERE!" Elayna called.

I blushed furiously, but there was no way anyone could have seen us from the cockpit.

Eivind pulled away. "Later?"

I grinned, pulled him in close to kiss his cheek, and whispered, "Later."

He sighed and adjusted himself, gesturing for me to go first. As I climbed the stairs up to the cockpit, Elayna craned around me to shout again: "EIVIND! THE CHAMPAGNE!"

Eivind rummaged for a few minutes and brought the bottle of chilled champagne up to the cockpit, where five plastic wineglasses waited.

"Captain," he said, and passed the bottle to Jonas.

Jonas removed the foil and untwisted the cage. Aiming the neck away from the cockpit, he pushed the cork and it came out with a loud pop, shooting overboard into the water. We all cheered and Jonas poured some bubbly into each glass.

Holding his glass up, he said, "Here is to the Pacific Ocean: her beauty is reputed to be the finest in the world. May her water and winds be sweet and kind. And here is to my crew: I could not have done it without you. Thank you for your help, and I'm glad to lead you onto our next adventure."

We clinked glasses, the sound dulled, but the champagne tasted so good.

"Okay, *mesdemoiselles et messieurs*, we have big plans for the evening," Elayna announced. "First stop, the rooftop!"

We downed our champagne and gathered at the side of *Eik*. Eivind pulled the line tied to the dinghy so that it was under the lifeline gate.

Jonas turned around and took a big step down to land in the dinghy. I watched Marcella and Elayna drop in; they were both wearing skirts, and they squatted down to sit on the edge of the deck, not minding their skirts riding up as their legs swung over the side. Then they slid off the edge to stand in the dinghy.

"A perk of the cruising life," Elayna said. "Sometimes you have to flash the captain."

Eivind offered me a hand. Thanks to my shorts, I didn't flash anyone. I sat on the tube next to Marcella while Eivind jumped down, line in hand. I traced my finger over the words painted onto the little boat: *Eikenøtt*.

My eyebrows drew together. "Little Oak?"

Eivind grinned. "Acorn."

We motored into the marina and to the dinghy dock, the inflatable riding low in the water with all of our weight. When we arrived, Eivind jumped out with the line, and I stood up and stepped onto the pontoon.

When we were all off, Eivind fixed the line to the cleat to secure the dinghy. Jonas pulled a small red cord off the outboard, silencing the engine. Attached to the cord was a small key, which he fitted to a lock and cable to prevent anyone from stealing the dinghy.

We walked through the marina to the road. La Playita Marina was located on a peninsula, a narrow strip of land connecting the marina to the rest of Panama City. Jonas and Eivind both pulled out their phones and requested Ubers.

Our Uber drivers took us to Casco Viejo, the old town of Panama City, and we got out in a square. Elayna led us through the lobby of a hotel and up the stairs to a rooftop bar. We grabbed a high top by the edge with a view of the coastline.

The scenery was stunning. The sun approached the horizon, the brightness of the day fading, and the lights of Panama City's skyscrapers, visible several kilometers down the coast, sparkled in the darkening sky.

While we waited for our drinks, Elayna pulled out her phone. "We *must* selfie." she said.

We gathered on one side of the table, the backdrop of the ocean and Panama City behind us.

"Un, deux, trois!"

Elayna took about fifteen pictures, the last half of which probably captured me grimacing. Eivind pulled back first.

"Enough, Elayna," he said, exasperated.

She let us break apart, but flipped through the photos. "Look. This one is perfect!" She thrust her phone in my face.

It *was* perfect. We were smiling, relieved and happy. The pastel light of early sunset gave the city a soft glow and the ocean extended off into the horizon.

In the picture, Eivind was by my side, one arm around my waist, the other on Jonas's shoulder, his palm squeezing his brother.

This might be the only picture I'd ever have with Eivind.

"Can you send this to me?"

"But of course."

When our drinks came, we clinked glasses.

"Tell me about where you'll go next," I said.

Eivind put his hand on my bare thigh and gave me a squeeze.

"From here," Jonas said as he traced a line in the air, demonstrating, "we sail southwest. We pass over the equator, and what is called the doldrums; there is no wind there. Then, when we find wind again, we turn west and sail until we hit the Marquesas."

Jonas told me more about the Marquesas, a cluster of island groups in French Polynesia— an overseas territory of France. They were the islands farthest to the east, and where sailors would make their first landfall after crossing the Pacific Ocean.

"How long will it take you to sail all that way?"

"Maybe twenty-five days. It depends on the doldrums."

"Wow, okay. And then what?"

"We will sail the islands a little bit: many small places in French Polynesia, including Tahiti and Bora

Bora, then the Cook Islands, Tonga, New Zealand. There I will sell the boat."

"How long will that take you?"

"We sail to New Zealand around November. That is where boats go to escape the cyclones."

"That will be an amazing trip. I'm so jealous of all the travel, but I'm not sure I could handle being on a boat for twenty-five days."

"Do you get seasick?" Eivind asked.

"A little. I've been on small boats before for day trips out in the ocean. It wasn't pleasant, but I didn't vomit. I guess you can't get seasick if you want to sail around like you are doing."

"That isn't true. I get seasick a little bit," Marcella told me. "I have thrown up once or twice, but it gets better after a few days. Plenty of sailors deal with it."

"It tends to get a little boring though," Eivind said. "You have to be able to entertain yourself for a long time."

"What's the longest you've been out at sea for?"

"Eivind and I," Jonas said, "with our other crew members, we did fourteen days across the Atlantic."

"And you?" I turned to Marcella and Elayna.

"I have sailed across the Atlantic, on a different boat before I met Jonas. It took us nineteen days at sea," Elayna said.

"My longest sail was on *Eik*, coming to Panama," said Marcella.

"That's amazing. Are you nervous?"

Marcella laughed. "Yes, of course. Everyone is on some level. I don't enjoy sailing much, but it's a good way to travel. Good for the environment and good for the soul, I think."

I nodded, trying to imagine what it would be like out there. Eivind's finger traced a small circle on my inner thigh and I tried not to get too distracted.

"What are the plans for tomorrow?"

"Well," Jonas said, leaning back, "I did check the weather forecast for this week, and we could leave on Monday."

"Really?" Eivind glanced at me. "That is sooner than we thought."

Jonas shrugged. "Yes, but we are ready. We need to stock up on food and do a few projects, but mostly I think it is time. Tomorrow we will do some more shopping, stuff like that."

"My flight is Monday too," I said.

"Where are you flying to?" Marcella asked.

"Bogotá, but I won't have much time in Colombia. I had to cut it short to make it through the canal with you."

"And then?"

"Peru, Ecuador, Bolivia, and Chile."

"Ah, along the Pan-American Highway. That is unfortunate that you will miss Argentina."

Marcella told me about a trip she took to Argentina, making me wistful for more time to add on a visit, and Eivind and Jonas talked about a project on the boat. A few people had started to sway to the music, and Elayna tried to convince Jonas to dance with her. When he couldn't be budged, Elayna stole Marcella instead.

Jonas stood up. "Hit the head," he explained.

Eivind and I were left alone at the table and his hand moved up my leg another inch. I tried to swat him away.

"Eivind, stop! I'm not going to make it very long if you keep teasing me."

"I don't want you to make it very long. I would rather spend an evening on the boat with you, doing anything, than drinking with my crewmates." He seemed to sober up a little bit. "We only have a few more days left."

"I know." I sighed. "It's kind of a good thing, bad thing, yeah?"

"What do you mean?"

"Well, four nights to have some fun," I said as I leaned around to kiss Eivind below his ear. "Not too short, not too long. You won't fall in love with me." I kissed him again and he snorted.

"Are you sure about that?"

"Stop it," I admonished him. "You know, I really like your neck too. Especially here." I traced my finger down his Adam's apple, and it bobbed as he swallowed.

A throat cleared behind me, and Jonas took a seat across from us.

Eivind held out his palm. "Keys."

Jonas groaned. "What? No! We have not even had dinner yet!"

"Sorry. Keys."

"You are *not* sorry."

"I am," I said.

"Trust me, you will not be," Eivind assured me. "Keys."

Eighteen

JONAS PULLED THE BOAT KEY AND THE CORD FOR THE dinghy out of his pocket and held them up in front of his face. "Promise me. When I call, you will come to pick us up. Eivind. Promise me."

"Yes, I promise."

"You will keep your phone on, plug it in when you get home, and make sure the ringer is on. PROMISE." Jonas turned to me. "Lila, promise."

I raised my right hand. "I solemnly swear I will not let rooting with Eivind strand you on land. This is not a mutiny."

Jonas rolled his eyes but handed the keys over to Eivind. "Move, move, move!" Eivind whisper-shouted like a commando as he guided me back into the stairwell.

We didn't make it more than half a flight down when Eivind pulled me against the wall and kissed my neck again.

"Eivind, honey, focus." I pulled his face away from mine. "I am not having sex in a stairwell."

"Right, yes. Fine." He winked as he tugged me along with him down the stairs.

Outside, we waited for our Uber to pick us up. I let Eivind kiss my neck again—I had never hooked up with a man so into necking. A thought occurred to me.

"Eivind, do you have protection?"

He pulled back a little bit. "Protection?"

"Condoms."

He smirked at me. "Yes, I have condoms."

"*Enough* condoms?"

He chuckled and pulled me close, his erection pressing against my thigh. "I have enough condoms to tire us both out. I promise."

Our Uber pulled up and we climbed in. Eivind snuggled with me in the back, touching and caressing my skin, heating me up even more. Respectful of our Uber driver, and aware we didn't have the cover of darkness yet, we kept our mouths to ourselves.

My brain had approached its limit, though, and I couldn't think of a proper conversation for the life of me.

We arrived at the dinghy dock and Eivind hopped into the little boat and put the cord in place.

"What can I do?" I asked.

He pulled the cord to start the engine and it fired to life.

"Untie the painter and hold it while you step in," he said, pointing at the line attaching the dinghy to the dock.

"The painter? Seriously? Fucking nautical words. Just call it another goddamn line." I untied while I grumbled. Eivind held out his hand and I awkwardly stepped down onto the tube of the dinghy. It bucked under me, a little less stable than I remembered, and I stumbled the rest of the way down. Eivind caught me before I went over the edge, but with the force of me falling and the weight of both of us on one side, it tipped dangerously low to the water.

"Whoa. Are you okay?"

"Yeah, sorry. I almost went swimming."

"Hold on to the painter—otherwise the water will pull it down under the boat and into the propeller."

Most. Complicated. Hookup. Of my life. Boat stuff still intimidated me, and feeling clumsy in addition to being intimidated put a damper on the sexy mood.

Eivind pushed away from the dock and put the engine in gear. We puttered toward *Eik*.

When the dinghy pulled up next to the boat, Eivind grabbed the railing on the deck and held us in place. I had to balance on the tube and take a big step to put my foot on the rail. Eivind put a hand under my butt to help me hoist myself up.

"If we give up now, at least my ass enjoyed some action."

Eivind handed me the line and I held it while he killed the engine and climbed on. He grabbed the painter from me and with his other hand pulled me close.

Between kisses on my neck and shoulder, he said, "I did not even try. Do not give up on me yet. I want a taste."

I shivered. "Yes, okay. I'm not giving up yet."

Eivind gave me a grin of victory. I waited in the cockpit while he led the dinghy back to the stern and secured her. He unlocked the companionway, slid the doors open, and disappeared into the dark.

I stepped carefully down. After having been up and down so many times, I'd gotten the hang of these stairs, like the rest of the crew. Enough light came in through the windows to illuminate Eivind waiting for me.

He didn't move as I stepped down further. I put my hands on his shoulders, intending to push him away so I could get off the stairs, but instead he grabbed my hips and pulled my body into his. I wrapped around him like an octopus and kicked my sandals off behind his back.

We stared at each other for a few moments. I pressed my forehead to his. "I think I should kiss you."

"You are not worried about getting kicked off the boat anymore?"

"Nope, now my greatest fear is exploding."

"Exploding?"

I nodded. "With lust."

"Obviously."

We both chuckled together, but our laughter died quickly. I zeroed in on Eivind's lips, pink and plump and perfect. They parted, waiting patiently for me to make a move.

I brushed my lips so slightly against his. We both breathed, still for a moment, before Eivind gripped me harder and my lips came crashing down onto his. Tasting each other, we made out with wild abandon.

Eivind started walking us to his cabin. I busied myself with showering his neck and ear with attention, kissing and nibbling as I went.

Kicking the door closed, Eivind moved toward the bed.

"Oh wait! Don't forget to plug in your phone."

Eivind grunted and unwrapped my legs from around his waist, tossing me playfully onto the bed. He pulled his phone out of his pocket and plugged it in, setting it on the small counter in the corner of his cabin. Turning back to me, he put a knee on the bedding between my legs and climbed up, holding his body over mine.

The curtains were open, and the dying light of the day shone in the room enough to see by. Eivind's eyes roamed my face, a serious look I'd never seen on him before. Then he tilted his head down.

Slowly, *finally*, his lips grazed mine again. The kiss was soft and gentle, just a moment of touching before he pulled back. He kissed me again and again, shifting to the corner of my mouth. When he came back, I let my lips part, and he took the invitation to kiss me deeper.

My hands were on his ribs, his in my hair. We kissed slow and languid, our tongues tasting each other. Eivind shifted, sliding his knees down and relaxing his lower body against mine. I gasped when his erection pressed into me, breaking the kiss.

Eivind chuckled and rocked against me gently. His mouth migrated to my neck, kissing my pulse point.

"You feel so good underneath me," he whispered.

I whimpered as he shifted the pressure and pulled my knee up to his waist. I rocked up to meet him, and we kissed again, deeper and hungrier.

Suddenly Eivind lifted off me. He pushed up onto his knees, and I was left spread and panting beneath him.

"Jesus," he said, running his hand over his head.

He got up from the bed and pressed a button on the fan nearby. Air flowed over my heated skin.

He rejoined me on the bed, putting his elbows on either side of my hips and pressing into me lower than he had before. A finger played with the strap of my cami and gently pushed it off my shoulder. He traced the edge, pulling the top down to expose my breast.

"The first time I saw you in a bikini," he said. "Do you remember?"

I nodded. "It was the first time I saw you shirtless."

He smiled, staring at my exposed nipple, and let his finger wander across my sensitive skin.

"I was hard the whole time. I had to keep my knees bent so no one would see. You are so beautiful."

Eivind leaned down and pressed his mouth to my breast, licking my nipple and closing his lips around it. I gasped and pressed my hips up into his chest. He nipped and sucked until I squirmed against him, my head thrown back and my eyes shut tight.

He let my breast go with a pop and then tugged my other strap down and began to play with my left breast. Eivind gave his attention wholeheartedly to my body, building me up until I had to pull him off me.

"Eivind," I panted. "Please. I need more."

His face broke into a wolfish grin and he pulled back onto his heels. Impatiently, he unsnapped the button of my shorts and yanked them and my knickers down together all at once. He tossed them over his shoulder and, with a palm on each of my thighs, pushed my legs apart.

Eivind staring at me hungrily was the sexiest thing I'd ever seen.

"I can't always cum from this," I blurted out.

His eyes shifted to look at me. "Okay."

"Okay."

He grinned and bent over, putting his mouth on me. My hips bucked against my will, and Eivind slid down further and wrapped his arms under my legs, palming my belly and sliding his tongue around, licking, kissing, and exploring. He teased my clit, touching and kissing but never lingering.

I writhed and encouraged him; he listened and soon pressure built low in my body.

"Oh God," I said.

Eivind closed his mouth over my clit and sucked lightly. My head pressed back against the bed, my eyes squeezed shut, and I focused on my body.

"Oh God. Eivind. Eivind. Suck harder, suck harder, suck harder," I chanted.

He did, and I fell apart, pulsing deep inside, my core clenching. Our eyes met for a moment, Eivind's piercing blue on fire in the dark shadows, but my eyes closed, my head fell back, and I went limp.

Nineteen

EIVIND GENTLY LET GO BUT KEPT HIS MOUTH PRESSED TO me, kissing me carefully. He worked down my inner thigh a little bit, and his hair prickled my skin as he rubbed his face against the sheet. He crawled up my body and we were eye to eye.

"Can I kiss you?"

I raised my head and put my lips on his before his words were even finished. I opened and tasted myself on him, letting our tongues slide together.

Eivind pulled away first. He sat on the edge of the bed and took his shirt off. Then he stood and finished stripping and reached over to a small cabinet on my left, one with a sliding door. He opened the door and pulled out a strip of condoms, then tossed them next to me on the bed.

He climbed back between my splayed legs and tore a condom off. His erection jutted out, hard and thick.

"Should I put this on?" he asked.

"Yes, please." I tried to take the condom from him to open it and put it on myself, but he backed away.

"I think it is better if I do it." He chuckled as he ripped the wrapper open and rolled the condom down his shaft. Holding himself above me, he placed a gentle kiss on my lips. "I will not last long. But I promise we will do it again, ja? If you feel okay."

I pulled his head down to kiss me again. "We have four days." We both grinned between kisses. "We can do more than that."

Eivind reached down and rubbed his hand against me, spreading the slickness. I shifted, trying to open myself up more to him, and he pressed his cock into me. He worked in carefully, stretching me a little as he went.

His hand came back up and his arms pressed into the bed on either side of me. His hips moved in shallow thrusts until he was all the way in, our bodies pressed tightly together.

We breathed.

We kissed.

Eivind rolled his hips and our lips broke apart, both of us panting.

"Goddamn it." Eivind laughed harshly. "I am so close already." He looked away, embarrassed.

I grabbed his face in both hands. "Eivind, look at me. You're going to fuck me again, right?"

His eyes rolled up and he groaned, thrusting into me again. "Yes."

"Promise me," I said.

His hips moved, dragging his cock in and out of me.

"Promise me you'll fuck me anytime I want."

He said something in Norwegian, but it started in a *ja*, so I took it as an affirmative. The muscles in his jaw clenched, his chin tucking down and his hips picking up speed. We were both sweating.

A few more thrusts and he bent over me, his body straining as he shouted into the bed. He twitched, pressed so deeply into me, and I hummed against his neck, stroking my fingers up and down his back.

We were quiet and still for a few moments. The boat rocked gently in the water.

Eivind inhaled and pulled back a little bit, taking some of his weight off me. He rained kisses on my neck and shoulder, eventually finding my lips and kissing me deeply. He was still inside me, and we stayed that way for a few minutes.

Finally he reached down and grabbed the base of the condom while he pulled out. He disappeared out the door and returned a few moments later, sans condom.

"Do you want to use the toilet or shower?"

"Yes, please." I rolled off the bed and cracked open the door. Hypothetically, I knew we were alone, but I poked my head out to be sure. Eivind laughed behind me.

I flicked the light on. Since most of the surfaces were white, I had to blink a few times to see properly. I peed and washed my hands before opening the door again.

Eivind sat on the bed, waiting for me.

"Are you sore?"

When I shook my head, he crooked a finger at me. "Come here."

I stood in front of him, between his legs. He traced a finger over my skin, leaving goose bumps in his wake. When his fingers slid down my stomach, I swayed toward him.

His hands were greedy and grabby, his cock hard again.

This time we were more frantic. We made out on the bed, hands building each other up until Eivind tore away to grab another condom. While he rolled it on, he asked, "What is your favorite position?"

Once the condom was on, I pushed him flat on his back and swung my leg over his hips. He grunted and grabbed my hips, his eyes a little wild.

"Fuck, yes."

I rode him, rocking my hips, playing with angles, enjoying his chest under my hands. Just as I started to hit the right spots, Eivind's phone rang. I groaned, slumping down to rest my forehead on Eivind's chest.

"You still really like your brother?" I said.

Eivind laughed. "Ja."

"Damn it. I do too."

I tried to get up, but Eivind gripped my hips and slammed me back down. The angle hit me deep and hard, making me shudder.

"Eivind."

He groaned and sat up. "I know."

He kissed me gently. The phone stopped ringing. He kissed me again. The ringing started back up.

This time when I moved, he didn't stop me. Eivind answered his phone and I admired his bare ass for the first time. He had a short discussion in Norwegian, looking at his watch, looking at me, and sighing. "Ja." He ended the call.

"Jonas?"

"Yes." Eivind took the condom off and disappeared into the bathroom. Water ran and he came back out and slipped on his shorts. "Please. Stay naked. Stay in my bed. Ja?"

I crawled up to the head of the bed and pulled the sheets over my naked body. "I'll be right here," I promised.

Eivind opened the door to his cabin and stepped out. Even though he couldn't see anything, his eyes raked over my body under the sheet. He groaned.

"One more peek?"

"Go!" I shouted at him, and he laughed before closing the door.

I didn't keep my promise, but only with our best interest at heart. I slid my camisole and underwear back on and quickly went to my cabin. I didn't think it was too presumptuous of me to assume I was staying the night with Eivind, so I grabbed some clothes for tomorrow and a few things I needed to put in Eivind's cabin. I brushed my teeth and properly washed my face, stripped off my clothes, and climbed back into Eivind's bed.

That was where I was when the rest of the group returned. Their laughter, their chatting, their footsteps, and only moments later Eivind came back in through the door.

"Hi," he whispered. "Still naked?"

"Of course," I replied. Eivind took his shorts off and climbed into bed next to me. I turned, pressing myself against his bare skin. "Do you want to go to sleep?"

"Hell no," Eivind breathed. "But we have to be quieter. Is that okay?"

"Mmmm . . . I'll try my best, but you feel so good." He kissed me for the compliment, and then we ground our bodies against each other. I circled my legs around his hips, letting his hardness rub against my softness until we were both slick and ready.

Eivind grabbed another condom and rolled it on. "Can I get on top again?" I asked.

Immediately he flopped onto his back. "I will never say no to you." He grinned.

I took control again, slipping him inside me and leaning forward onto my hands, grinding our hips together. We were quieter and slower this time, just the sound of our breathing filling the room.

"Put your knees up," I said.

Eivind obliged, and I leaned back instead, shifting my hips forward and rolling against him. Soon I was panting as quietly as I could, tension building inside me.

Eivind strained under me, and I brought my fingers to where our bodies met. Eivind watched, enraptured.

Suddenly I was at the edge. "Eivind!" I said a little too loudly.

He sat up, placing a hand on the back of my head and another over my mouth.

"Come for me, darling. I want to feel it."

I climaxed and shuddered, whimpering beneath his palm. Tears welled up as I kept my fingers going, dragging it out for as long as I could. Finally I collapsed against him, and he moved his hands and guided me back down, laying me on top of him, boneless and fluid.

"Do you mind if I . . . ?"

"Please do." I sighed and snuggled into him. Eivind lifted his hips, thrusting up into me. I put my hands on his abdomen and his muscles flexed and contracted under me. He built up a rhythm, slowly and quietly winding himself up.

With a muffled cry, his body curved and he came, gritting his jaw and grunting.

We both collapsed back, happy and spent. Eivind kept his hands on me for a few minutes, tracing up and down my back.

"Do you want to clean up first?" he asked me.

I nodded and heaved myself off his body. We cleaned up and Eivind brushed his teeth. I was drowsy when he came back to bed and slipped in behind me. He rested an arm on my waist, and the last thing I remember was a lazy kiss and a whispered good night.

Twenty

I WOKE UP TO AN ERECTION PRESSED AGAINST MY ASS AND warm lips on my neck. I mumbled a good morning.

Now that Eivind knew I was awake, he reached down between my legs and worked me up. I reminded myself to keep quiet, to stifle my moans in the pillow.

Eivind rolled away, a cool breath of air rushing in, and then he returned, wrapped in a condom. He slid my top leg forward and, holding himself up on one arm, pushed into me. A little soreness lingered, but Eivind was careful and gentle. Once we got into a rhythm, he reached in again and brought me to climax, my body clenching around his cock.

A few more thrusts and he tipped over the edge too, groaning into my skin. We both caught our breath and Eivind slipped out to clean up.

We dozed for a while, the boat rocking and swaying under us. At one point, Eivind's hands were on me again.

"No more." I pushed his hand away. "Three times is enough! What are you, a machine?"

Eivind chuckled and pulled me close. "Three may have been too much, yes? I promise, only cuddling now."

When I woke up again, Eivind was dressing. I pulled the duvet over my head and tried to go back to sleep.

"What, are you not a morning person?" Eivind teased, tugging at the cover. "Lila," he said, groping my butt. "At least go clean up."

"I know, I know," I said, my voice muffled.

He patted my ass before he left. So Eivind was a morning person.

I finally threw the cover off and made myself get up. The smells coming from the galley were too good to ignore, and the voices had grown louder now that they weren't worried about waking us up.

I threw on some shorts and a tank top and ducked into the head to clean up.

Marcella and Elayna were in the galley, frying batches of toast. Jonas already had his laptop out on the table and was drinking some coffee. Eivind sat on the couch, wolfing down some toast with jam.

Marcella spotted me first. Her face lit up and she walked over to give me a hug. I blushed.

"You had a good night?" she whispered.

"Yeah." I released her and my eyes immediately went to Eivind, who wore a big grin. He swallowed a bite of toast as I slid onto the couch next to him. He pulled me closer.

"Hey, baby," he said, and kissed me, softly at first, but then he licked and deepened the kiss. He pulled back when a kitchen towel flopped over our heads. Eivind chuckled and tossed the towel back at Elayna, who smiled but didn't respond.

Jonas caught my eye as he sipped his coffee. He smiled, genuinely happy for his brother.

Elayna gave me a plate and I helped myself to some toast and sliced fruit from the platter. Next came a round of coffee for me and Eivind.

I asked about their evening, and Marcella told me about rooftop barhopping; they had been to three other roofs as the night went on, but they said everything was pretty low-key since it had been a Wednesday night.

Elayna was unusually quiet and slipped upstairs to eat in the cockpit instead of down with us. Jonas was still working on his laptop, and Eivind ate as if the sex had dug a bottomless pit in his stomach.

Marcella and I chatted about her plans for the day. She and Elayna were going to the supermarket to stock up for the passage. Jonas had an errand to run to pick up supplies (he was looking for something he called a joker valve), so they agreed to head to shore together.

"What do you want to do today?" Eivind asked me.

"You don't have any chores?" I said.

Eivind looked at Jonas, who said, "Not today, but first thing tomorrow morning we must go up the mast."

"Ja," Eivind agreed, and looked at me. "I am yours today."

"Well, we could go do the canal visitor center or go see the ruins of Panamá Viejo?"

"I would like to see the canal museum."

I smiled. "That sounds good."

Everyone parted ways to get ready, and I returned to my small cabin to dress properly for the day.

When we were all ready to go, we piled into the dinghy and puttered to shore, hailing three Ubers at the marina and splitting up.

Our drive out to the museum took twenty-five minutes. It was at the Miraflores lock we had passed through the day before.

Eivind and I wandered into the museum and learned about the history of the Panama Canal, reading about the original attempts to build it, the death toll for every year of construction, the battles for control. I used my phone to snap photos of tidbits and facts.

"What are you doing?" Eivind asked.

"I'm going to send some of these to my dad. He's been super excited about my trip and has been reading books and watching all these TV shows about the canal. He'd like seeing this."

Eivind cocked his head. "Your dad is an engineering nerd like you?"

"Worse than me." I grinned. "He's why I got my engineering degree." We moved to the next display, which showed a model of a Panamax ship.

"But you do not work as an engineer?"

"Not yet."

Eivind studied the model. "Right. Not yet."

"When I get back to Australia, I'll find a job. What about you? Do you want to go home when this trip is over?"

"Yes, Jonas and I will move back to Norway."

"What about work?"

Eivind sighed and ran his hand over his head. "I might get my job at the restaurant back."

"Oh." I couldn't imagine having so few plans in life. It killed me not to be able to interview for jobs yet, but it would be too complicated while traveling. "You don't want to do something with your degree?" I peered into a display to look at a diorama of the construction of the canal.

"No."

I waited a moment, but Eivind didn't elaborate.

We took seats in the theater to catch a cheesy fifteen-minute video about the canal, complete with an animated mascot and nineties soundtrack.

Then we went to the highlight: the shaded bleachers overlooking the lock. We sat and watched—you could even buy popcorn—as several rounds of boats came and went. Sailboats similar to *Eik* came through with more drama than we experienced. Sometimes we were sure they were going to hit another boat during their maneuvers.

Watching while outside of the canal made it easier to see the process of pulling and stopping the big ships, and we could watch the mules and the crew of the canal work to position everyone.

Eivind kicked his feet up on the seats in front of us. Out of over a hundred seats, we had the place mostly to ourselves. While in the stands, Eivind looped his arm over my shoulders.

"We should go out to dinner tonight."

"Look at you, all fancy, wanting to take me out on a date," I said.

"We did miss out on the sunset and dinner last night. So tonight let us go, just the two of us."

"That sounds good. I don't have many nice clothes, so I'll have to wear the same thing I wore last night. Backpacker problems."

"I do not care what you wear," he said. "As long as you are with me."

I smiled and gave him a quick kiss on the lips, and we resumed watching the ship traffic.

———————

I SIPPED A COCKTAIL AT OUR TABLE. WE SAT AT A different rooftop bar in Casco Viejo, no less beautiful than the one last night. Eivind and I had arrived about an hour before, and I was on my second mojito of the night. We'd had a stellar view of the sunset and now the skyline was lighting up as daylight faded.

"So, how many girls like me have you hooked up with?" I asked.

Eivind once again looked sexy in shorts and a polo shirt. His sunglasses sat on top of his head.

"Like you? None."

"Smooth."

He grinned.

"I'm really curious. It seems like, being single, there would be a lot of casual sex going around."

"No. In the Caribbean there were a few places where superyacht crews, like Marcella's, hung out and partied together. But the cruisers . . . most of them are married and older. There are a few single crew members here and there, and I think we have met one or two female solo sailors, but no, there have not been many opportunities."

"So, with Elayna and Jonas, is it the opportunity, or . . . ?"

Eivind grunted. "I am not sure. For Elayna, maybe she really does like him. But they do not seem to be on the same page sometimes. Jonas is a . . ." Eivind waved his hand, looking for his words. "He likes to stay at home. Elayna, I do not think she sees how he tires out sometimes."

I hummed and thought about it. "Nah, yeah. I can see that. There is no one waiting back home for either of you?"

"No," Eivind said, smiling. "I am all yours. As for my brother, his wife left him a few years ago."

"Right, I remember you said he was divorced." I cocked my head. "Did you like her?"

He hesitated. "I did. But I think I was a little blind to her. Looking back, after seeing how hurt Jonas was when she left . . ." He shook his head. "I still don't really know why she left. I do not understand it."

"That must be hard for Jonas."

"It was maybe the first time I saw my brother as just a man. He needed to do something different, to find happiness. He loved sailing as a kid, so I could see that this would be a chance for him to recover and move on."

"You are a good brother."

"Thank you."

"And you are good at other things, too."

Eivind pinched my thigh under the table, and our waiter appeared with our food. We ate and talked, learning more about each other.

After dinner, we strolled through Casco Viejo, the old town of Panama City.

"Did you know this is the second capital?"

Eivind shook his head. "How many are there?"

"Old Panama City was the first, burned down by Captain Morgan. Casco Viejo is the second, and modern

Panama City is the third. The first city was founded in 1519."

"That is very old for the New World, ja?"

I nodded. "That's before a European ever set foot in Straya."

We walked up and down the streets. It was night, but Casco Viejo was one of the popular tourist destinations, so it was still busy. The buildings surrounding us were old, colorful examples of Spanish colonial architecture.

"This is what I imagine Havana must be like."

Eivind nodded toward an open storefront. "I bet Havana doesn't have that."

It was a shop selling nothing but ice blocks—or Popsicles, as Eivind called them. The ice blocks were beautiful—kiwis and lemon slices glinted under their icy coats, and exotic flavors were available. Eivind ordered guava cheesecake and I went with classic strawberry. We walked to the shore and tried not to let the ice blocks drip on our hands while we ate.

Casco Viejo was surrounded by an elevated highway that circled the old city. Once the highway joined land again, pedestrians could cross the road and walk along the shore. With the last of our Popsicles, we walked along the sidewalk, which was called the Cinta Costera.

In front of us lay the glittering lights of modern Panama City. Behind us, the softer lights of the old town. To our right stretched the dark, inky Pacific Ocean.

"I can't believe you are going to sail away."

"Sometimes I can't believe it either."

"How do you afford to do this?"

Eivind stopped us and gazed out over the ocean, the horizon visible in the moonlight. "Jonas supports me."

I looked up at Eivind, his face unreadable in the shadows. "That's nice of him."

"He has done very well for himself in his job, and needed a crew member." Eivind looked down at me. "It was a win-win for both of us."

I stretched up to kiss his cheek, and he smiled faintly before turning back to look out over the ocean.

Twenty-One

I WOKE UP ALONE IN THE MORNING, DIM LIGHT SHINING through the window onto the tousled bed. I vaguely remembered Eivind leaving me, and wondered what had woken me up.

I stretched and recalled last night: coming "home" to the boat, tumbling into bed together, tender kisses and quiet moans.

Something thumped over my head, then another thump, and the sounds of footsteps walking down the deck.

I slipped my pajamas on and headed into the main salon. Marcella, bleary-eyed this early, wordlessly offered me a cup of coffee and I climbed up to the cockpit and into the morning. I leaned out the canvas enclosure and found Eivind and Jonas at the mast. Jonas strapped himself into a harness, which attached to a line going all the way up to the top of the mast.

Eivind checked the harness and the lines, preparing Jonas as if he were belaying a rock climber. He was shirtless, wearing a pair of board shorts and a set of sailing gloves. When he was satisfied, he moved around to the winch, heaved the line around it, and the lines attached to Jonas tightened.

Eivind put a handle on the winch and started to crank. His bare back was to me, and I watched the muscles flex and release with each crank.

I was so distracted by Eivind that at first I didn't notice Jonas rising up off the deck. He used all four of his limbs to grip the mast as he rose.

"No way." I gasped, shading my eyes to watch as Jonas climbed higher and higher. It started to hurt my neck, staring up and craning to see. I looked down at Eivind and he was watching Jonas too, breaking into a sweat while cranking the winch.

My eyes went back to Jonas. He approached the top of the mast thirty meters up in the air. When he reached out with a closed fist, Eivind stopped cranking.

"Hey, darling." Eivind winked at me and gave me a naughty grin.

"Morning." I sauntered over and gave him a kiss. Sipping from my mug, I sat down on the deck near the base of the mast. "What's he doing up there?"

"He is checking the rigging. We do this before every big passage: check the lines, the stays, the blocks. We make sure she is strong and ready to sail."

I let Eivind stand and watch his brother with silent focus. After a few minutes Jonas gave a hand signal and Eivind took the handle off of the winch. Carefully, he gripped the line while unwinding it, and I watched as Jonas was lowered slowly down. He gave the fist signal again, and Eivind wrapped the line around the winch to hold it.

They repeated this several times, Jonas going lower and lower every time. When he was low enough, I could see what he was doing. He stopped at every fixture and wire on the mast, and from a pocket in his harness he withdrew several items. He had a flashlight to shine into the shadows, his phone to take pictures, and a few tools I couldn't identify from where I stood.

Finally Eivind lowered Jonas all the way down to the deck.

"How is everything?" Eivind asked.

"Good. She looks good. I see no problems."

I smiled into my mug and watched the two brothers talk more about shrouds and antennae and other boat parts I didn't understand.

"Now that project is done," Eivind said, "breakfast time."

We sat down in the main salon together as Marcella finished preparing breakfast. This morning she'd made us a quiche with lardons and spinach.

The crew all talked about their plans, the things they needed to do before they took off across the ocean. Marcella and Elayna were going to buy more food, and Eivind was in charge of refilling their cooking gas tank.

Jonas drove everyone to shore in the dinghy, leaving me alone on the boat for a few minutes. I tucked myself into Eivind's cabin and called my dad.

"Sweet pea, it's so good to hear from you."

"Thanks, Dad! I'm not calling too late, am I?"

"No, it's fine. Your mum's gone to bed, but I'm up watching the late news and working on my puzzle."

Dad had found a Panama Canal puzzle to do while I was here.

"I loved the pictures you sent me yesterday. Some of those facts are really interesting, and of course, some are contrary to what I've learned from my shows. I will have to do some research to try to find the truth."

I told Dad more about the museum the day before and the past few days in Panama City, and that I was still staying on *Eik*.

"You spent the day with Eivind yesterday?"

"Yep."

"Dinner too, eh?"

"Yes, Dad."

"If this guy is spending all day with my daughter, I think I deserve to know what he looks like. Just in case."

I rolled my eyes. "I'll send you a picture. We took some photos yesterday."

"That's my girl."

When I was off the phone with Dad, I spent a few minutes tidying up the few personal effects I had around Eivind's room.

I wandered into the cockpit to look for Jonas. He sat in the shade, a black bucket at his feet and an old towel spread out on the bench.

"Hallo," he said. "How are your parents?"

"Good. Dad said to say thank you for letting me go through the canal with you."

Jonas smiled at me. "They are welcome. You were a good crew."

"Even if I didn't do anything?" I grinned.

Shrugging, Jonas said, "Everybody did something. You may not have handled lines, but you helped where you could. It is hard to throw people together in close places, but having you here has been good."

"Thank you. What are you doing?"

"This is the winch." He pointed to the bucket. I peered in and at the bottom was a collection of metal parts, gears, and pins, covered in a layer of water: the guts that made the winch work. "It needs to be taken apart and cleaned every so often. This one I had not had time to clean before the canal."

"Can I help?" I asked.

"Sure. Take a rag here, and take a part out of the bucket and clean and dry it. Then lay it here on the towel."

"What's in the bucket?"

"Baking soda and vinegar. There is grease on many of the parts, and it helps to cut the grease."

"Cool," I said. I picked up one of the pieces and began to work, using my short fingernails wrapped with the rag to clean the old black grease out of the gears.

"What about you? What do you think of the crew?" Jonas finished cleaning a piece and set it down on the towel between us.

"Well, I like Eivind."

Jonas snorted. "I heard."

My face went scarlet. "Oh. My. God. We try to be quiet!"

"Lila." Jonas laughed. "It is not that bad. We live on a boat, there is only so much space, and we get used to very little personal distance pretty quickly. It happens."

"Still. That's mortifying. I didn't realize you were such a perv, Jonas."

He laughed again.

"Honestly, it kind of surprises me to have as little drama as you do. Especially with a bunch of young, attractive single people." We both went quiet. "What about you and Elayna?" I asked him.

Jonas sighed. "Nothing. We have not done anything in a while."

I hummed in sympathy.

"Actually," Jonas started. "Would you be okay with moving into Eivind's room? And Elayna can go back to her bunk?"

"Yeah, no worries. Sorry about that."

Jonas waved a hand. "It is okay. But maybe it is best if Elayna and I do not share a room anymore."

I nodded. "Well, I'm sorry to be saying goodbye so soon. I guess that's part of the cruising life, right? Moving on to the next place."

Jonas studied my face. "Do you like my brother enough to stay?"

"Yes, of course I do! He's fun and a good person and I like the way he treats me."

"But you will not stay?"

My brain tripped for a moment. "Wait, 'stay' as in, sail across the Pacific with you?"

"Ja."

"Honestly, I didn't think that was possible."

Jonas didn't look up from his work. "Why not? I told you to stay as long as you wanted to."

I rolled my eyes. "There's a difference between staying a few days here in Panama and committing to a month out at sea together. Plus, like, yes, I appreciate the offer, but I don't know how Eivind feels about that."

A skeptical eyebrow popped up. "Really?"

I blushed again.

"You should ask him."

We continued our work in silence while I thought about the possibility of sailing across the ocean. After having met so many people, boat owners like Peter and Edith or hitchhikers like Elayna and Marcella, I realized this was a golden opportunity. If I wanted to experience something that would be life-changing and so different from the life I would go home to in Australia, this was that opportunity. Shouldn't I take it?

And yet it terrified me. All of my detailed plans would be tossed overboard. Yes, I enjoyed every moment with Eivind: he was bright, funny, and so kind that he made my heart ache. But I'd never lived with a guy, never crossed so many boundaries that we would encounter while out at sea.

And yet, if I could make it across the Pacific Ocean and still feel so strongly about him, wouldn't this be something worth keeping?

Jonas and I kept working and talked about other things. I was delighted when he let me put the winch back together, following the exploded view in the manual.

When the winch was reassembled and working properly, I packed my things up from the bunk cabin and moved them into Eivind's room. I tucked them into a corner, trying to take up as little space as I could.

Marcella and Elayna returned first, and I helped them unload the provisions into the galley and put things away as best I could. When we were done, I retreated to the room to read until Eivind got back.

Raised voices carried through the door, and I opened it to see what was going on. Marcella was in the galley, mixing some dough for biscuits, and shot me a look. The argument came from the aft cabin—Jonas's room. It sounded a little one-sided: Elayna's voice was emotional and desperate, while Jonas's was calm but insistent.

I ducked back into the room.

Later that afternoon, Elayna moved her items back into the bunk cabin.

Twenty-Two

LATER THAT NIGHT I LAY IN BED, LETTING MY HEART RATE slow down. Eivind sprawled next to me, catching his breath after another session between the sheets. We'd gotten better at keeping quiet, and anytime I had been too tempted to let out a moan, my conversation with Jonas drifted into my head and I bit my tongue.

I turned to look at Eivind. He was flat on his back, legs splayed out and an arm over his face. I would have thought he was falling asleep, but his other hand was in mine, running a thumb over my knuckles.

I licked my lips. "Eivind?"

"Yeah?" came a muffled response.

"I had a conversation with Jonas today."

Eivind moved his arm to look at me.

"He told me I could stay as long as I wanted on the boat."

"Yes, I remember that."

"No, like, *as long as I wanted*. Like, across the Pacific with you all."

He grinned at me. "Are you thinking about it?"

I huffed at him. "That's not exactly an invitation from you, is it? Do you even want me to come?"

Eivind propped himself up on his arm and leaned down, pressing his nose to mine. "Lila, come sail across an ocean with me."

I shoved him away and he grunted as he hit the bed. "Seriously, that's it? You both are so casual about this like it's not a huge deal that you are inviting me to join you all to sail across an ocean. Do you know how ridiculous that is?"

Eivind sat up. "I know it is a big deal. But what is the worst that could happen?"

"I could be a murderer! I could break your boat!"

"That you worry about those things makes me trust you. We trust you. It is the people who are careless who I worry about. You are not careless. I trust you because I see you understand the value of these things: our lives, our boat, our stuff. You are interested in it all and curious and thirsty to know more. Most people would be scared to do this thing, but it does not paralyze you. Someone who has made a commitment like you have, to

188

do these things that you want to do, you do not let yourself be stilled by it." He touched my cheek. "Lila, this is what I like about you. You are brave and happy, and you have come onto this boat and I like how independent you are. That is why I would want you to stay."

I swallowed, a hunk of emotions in my throat.

"I know, though, that you have things you wanted to do. You may not want to push off your plans to go to South America and travel. I do not want to make it seem like they are the same adventures—they are not. This is harder. But yes, of course I want you to come."

"You don't think it's crazy that we've only known each other two weeks and I'd go sail across an ocean with you?"

"It is crazy." He grinned and pulled me onto his lap. "I am a little crazy. You are a little crazy. What do you think is the crazy part? Is it us, and that we are sleeping together? Or is it the sailing part?"

I leaned into Eivind's arms. "Both?"

"Okay. Sailing a boat offshore is safer than riding in a car. You are more likely to die in a car accident than out in the ocean."

"Really?"

He nodded.

189

"Statistically proven?"

He nodded again. "Now, say we broke up. There are—"

"Wait," I interrupted. "If we broke up? I wasn't aware we were dating."

"Well, no. But if you say yes to sailing across the ocean with me, you will say yes to being my girlfriend."

"Oh, is that how it works? Okay, Mr. I Have It All Planned Out, what happens if we break up?"

"I will let you have the whole boat. Unless I am on watch, I will stay in my cabin—I usually do anyway—and you will barely see me. I know the rest of the crew would still like having you around."

I sighed. "Well, it's not a perfect plan, but I appreciate it."

Eivind kissed my head and leaned us back onto the mattress. "Is that a yes?"

"Let me think about it. I'd have to delay my flight again."

"We would need to go buy some supplies for you."

"Like what?"

"You need a harness, maybe some gloves, and more food. Stuff like that."

"Hmm." Combined with the canceled flight, this might be too expensive for me. I studied Eivind's face carefully. "What about when we get there? What happens then?"

"If we are still together?" he teased.

I turned my head and playfully bit Eivind's pec. "Yes, if we are still together."

He was quiet for a moment, lightly stroking my arm. "I have to stay on *Eik*, you know this?"

A nasty little feeling rose in my gut, even though he was just confirming what I already expected. "Right," I said quickly. "And I would fly over here again and still have some time to backpack."

He hummed. "We can talk more about it tomorrow. For now, go to sleep."

"Wait, wait. One more thing."

"Ja?"

"What's the deal with Jonas and Elayna? I mean, it was pretty bad today, right? Do they fight a lot?"

My head rose and fell with Eivind's sigh. "No, they do not normally fight like this. My brother can be a bit dense about women sometimes."

I grinned into the darkness. "How so?"

"Elayna was interested in him early on. I think he was too focused on his responsibilities to pay attention to her, but she was waiting. And I know that my brother

191

gets lonely—we all do. So, one night, a couple months ago, she made a move at a little bar in Antigua."

"It's surprising to me that Jonas wouldn't have been paying attention to her. She's very pretty."

"He was different after the divorce. More unsure of himself. And he already felt like he had to work hard, I think. After our dad left, he was the man of the house, and taking care of our mother and me was his job."

"Sounds like he grew up fast."

"Ja. I want him to enjoy this trip. Maybe it will help him loosen up."

"And Elayna?"

"I like Elayna, but not for my brother. I hope she's able to move on."

We snuggled into bed together, and I listened to Eivind's breathing even out and deepen while I pressed against his chest. My mind raced, though, too energized to sleep. This was a huge commitment to make, not just to my travel plans, but to Eivind. What had started as a fling was ballooning out of control. I tried to consider my options, but I didn't have enough information. I carefully pulled away from Eivind and rolled to the other side to pick up my phone.

I quickly found that there were airports in the Marquesas Islands, and they connected to Tahiti, which connected everywhere.

Opening my spreadsheet, I used the tiny screen to scroll around and readjust my schedule. Could I still visit all five countries? I had already cut a week out of Colombia, but to sail across the Pacific, I would have to cut a month.

Gone was the side trip to the Galápagos, which helped my budget significantly. I cut out Colombia completely. I could use a fraction of that money to book a group tour on the Inca trail. I thought about Marcella's stories of Argentina and wondered if it would be cheaper to fly from Bolivia to Buenos Aires instead of to Santiago.

On a notepad on my phone, I started to write out some questions and make some lists. What would I need to survive life at sea for a month?

Twenty-Three

IT TURNED OUT, JUST LIKE GOING THROUGH THE CANAL, I would mostly be along for the ride. Bleary-eyed from staying up too late, I ran over my questions and concerns with Jonas in the morning during breakfast.

"Would I take a shift?"

"Yes, we will give you one shift, two hours every afternoon."

"So everyone else divides up twenty-two hours? That doesn't seem fair."

He shrugged. "Four or five hours a day is nothing. We could sail the boat just me and Eivind if we wanted to."

"What about chores?"

"Marcella cooks. Clean your room, keep a good watch, and I will be happy."

"You make it sound so easy."

He grinned at me. "It is."

Marcella told me if I was going to join them, I should run to the supermarket and stock up on any personal effects I would need for a month or two and whatever kind of munchies I wanted. She said they had a lot of food—the fridge and freezer were full of vegetables and meat, but Marcella would have to stock up on more canned goods to feed an extra person.

"What will I need to pay for?" I asked.

Jonas and Eivind looked at each other. Eivind answered. "Thirty dollars a week for groceries. If you want to buy anything special for yourself, then keep it in the cabin with you."

That was less than I had planned to spend.

"I could book a flight out of Tahiti on April first. This might work."

Jonas shook his head. "We *think* we will get in by April first, but we might not. Plus, you have to fly to Tahiti from Hiva Oa. You would have to just cancel your flight if you came with us. I am sorry, Lila, but I cannot let you keep us on a schedule."

"Oh." I deflated a little bit. I would have to cancel my flight, and all of these plans I had in South America, and would have no idea when I could resume my schedule.

I reran my budget over again and trimmed my schedule down even more. Now, instead of three months exploring South America, I was looking at a measly three-week vacation, enough time to visit two or three countries.

Like the day before, we split up to accomplish various tasks. I headed to shore with Elayna and Marcella to tackle our laundry situation. With the bare minimum clothes I had, I needed to do laundry often, but I usually washed my things by hand. Combined with the laundry for all five of us, though, it made much more sense to head to a laundromat. *Eik* even had a community laundry budget tucked away in a bag of coins. Jonas told me to throw my minuscule pile of laundry in with everything else.

Since *Eik* was about to set out to sea, it was the last chance for laundry—everything had to be washed. That meant we struggled and tripped over eight large trash bags full of laundry: all the dirty clothes, pillows, sheets, towels—anything that could be washed was in our bags. And we had to pull those bags up onto *Eik*'s deck, into the dinghy, out of the dinghy, then carry them down the dock, shove them into an Uber, and lug them from the Uber to the laundromat.

We were sweaty and gasping with laughter by the time we arrived. We worked quickly, dividing the laundry between multiple machines, then settled down into chairs to wait.

Immediately we all pulled out our phones. I was still trying to finalize my budget and itinerary, growing increasingly frustrated by the limitations of a small screen.

A few minutes later Elayna sniffled.

Marcella and I exchanged concerned looks over Elayna's head. I squeezed Elayna's shoulder. "Hey . . ." I crooned at her.

"Désolée," she said, sniffing again and wiping a tear on her cheek. "I was just chatting with my girlfriend and telling her that . . . Jonas and I are not . . ." She struggled with her words. I looked at Marcella, wide-eyed. She pulled out a tissue and handed it to Elayna.

Elayna dabbed her eyes with the tissue. "You and Eivind are so cute, but Jonas has never been interested in me like that. In the two months since we first slept together, it's been more about needs and loneliness than romance. To go on a date . . ."

"I'm sorry," I whispered, and pulled her in for a side hug.

Marcella rubbed her back. "I am sorry too, Elayna. What can we do?"

"Ah, this is nothing. I just feel foolish. Jonas has always been like this. I thought maybe when I stayed in his cabin, things would change, but they have not. It was never like that for him."

"But you like him a lot?"

"Yes."

I chewed on my bottom lip. "Is it bad enough that you would leave *Eik*?"

Elayna sat up with a bit more determination this time. "No. It is sad, but I will just have a cry over it and move on. I want to cross the Pacific, and it would be even more foolish to give up an opportunity like this."

"Good," Marcella said. "I am glad. It would not be the same without you."

"I want to talk about something else. Lila, do you think you will sail with us?"

"I don't know. It's not just extending a few days; it really changes my whole plan."

"Yes, it is a commitment."

"You both are more well traveled than I am—what would you do? Cross the Pacific or stick with my original plan?"

Marcella scrunched up her nose in thought. "Hmm . . ."

"They are very different," Elayna said.

"Yes," Marcella agreed. "Backpacking in South America is challenging, but so is sailing. In different ways." She sighed. "It is hard to understand how great of an opportunity this is to sail with Jonas and Eivind. The boat is amazing, and I trust Jonas completely as a captain. This is the whole package, and that is very hard to come by."

"Argh! How can I make this choice?"

Marcella laughed. "Oh no, I have a gorgeous, hunky man who wants to have me trapped on a boat with him for a month."

"Well, when you put it like that." I huffed at her.

"I do not want to downplay how hard it will be," Elayna said. "But these islands we are going to, this is a lifelong dream for most people."

"Nah, yeah. I guess I should learn to be more flexible. I just hate that I took *so much time* to research and plan this trip and now it is for nothing."

"You are young," Marcella said. "There is plenty of time to travel. You will have the opportunity to go to South America again."

"Yeah, but I will have a job. I hope."

"And more money," Marcella countered.

"True."

"How are things with you and Eivind?" Elayna asked.

"We don't have to talk about that," I said.

"It is okay. I want to hear your love story."

I blushed and laughed. "I doubt it's love."

Marcella raised her eyebrows. "I can see it happening. Eivind flirts but he is genuine. He has not been this interested in anyone that I've seen."

"Good," I said, and the girls laughed.

"Eivind has always been kind of . . ." Elayna trailed off.

"Independent?" Marcella suggested.

Elayna wiggled her head. "He is himself. He is contained. Jonas has always been the opposite. He has always been looking for something."

"Yeah, but that's kind of the thing," I said. "If I sail across the ocean with him, that's a big deal. We'd be sharing his cabin and all these experiences. But then I'd leave, and . . ." I hesitated for a moment. "Eivind would just go back to being his independent self, and where would I be?"

Marcella eyed me. "Back in Australia?"

"Oh, right." I picked at my fingernail while lost in thought for a moment. Then I threw up my hands. "See? Only a couple of weeks with Eivind and I'm having all kinds of insane thoughts. What would happen after a month together out at sea? I'd be hopeless."

It was Elayna's turn to comfort me now. She squeezed my shoulders and I leaned against her for a moment.

"I remind myself every day," Elayna said, "that this is an amazing adventure. I'm here to make the most of the time I have."

Twenty-Four

IT WAS TIME FOR A LATE LUNCH WHEN WE GOT BACK TO the boat. We gathered in the main salon, and Marcella set some large platters on the table.

"Make-your-own sandwiches," she announced.

I made a sanger and picked at it while the conversation flowed around me. I needed to make a decision.

Eivind finished his second sanger as I sat down. "What do you think, darling?"

I took a deep breath. As our clothes had been drying, I'd made a pros and cons list, which never failed to help me think straight. "I'm thinking yes. It's crazy, but yeah, why not, right? When will I ever get the chance to do this again?"

He smiled broadly and pulled me under his arm. "I think you will like it."

While we ate, Jonas went over a watch schedule that made everyone relatively happy and a departure checklist, assigning tasks to each crew member.

Marcella walked me through the galley, showing me where she stored snacks that were for everyone, plus ginger snaps and cream crackers.

"For seasickness," she explained. "It's good to have things on hand. I get seasick if the conditions are bad enough, but that's normal. When the weather is rough on board, no one is comfortable, not even Jonas."

Eivind and Marcella took me to the supermarket to help me buy supplies for the trip. I walked up and down every single aisle of the store, putting items in my cart. Deodorant, toothpaste, tampons, more underwear. The list went on and the cart piled up.

"Where am I going to store all this stuff?" I asked Eivind.

"There is room in my cabin."

"I guess so. Just don't kick me out of bed—I'll have to rearrange everything. Do we need more condoms?"

Eivind peered at the display and looked over the choices. I did some math in my head, but apparently so did Eivind. He grabbed five boxes—one hundred condoms—and threw them in the cart.

"One hundred?" I said. "You want *one hundred* condoms?"

"Yes."

I waited, but he didn't elaborate. "Why do we need one hundred condoms?"

He winked at me and continued down the aisle. "So you do not get pregnant."

I took a deep breath and held it for a moment, debating whether I wanted to say anything or not.

Eivind eyeballed me. "Are you mad?"

"No." I let out my breath. "I was thinking . . . I'm on birth control. I got six months' worth before I left Straya"

Eivind stopped walking. "Are you saying you do not want to use condoms?"

"Well . . . we leave in three days. That's probably not enough time to get tested, is it?"

Eivind thought for a moment. "I think we should stick with condoms. It does make cleaning up easier."

"Nah, yeah, that's fair."

One fully loaded cart later, we arrived at the checkout. We stacked up all of my items on the conveyor belt for the cashier and when it was time to pay, I cringed as I handed over my credit card. I reminded myself that these things would last me for over a month, and it was better to be safe than sorry—if I ran out, there was nowhere to resupply.

Eivind bagged up my stuff with the reusable bags he had brought. We stacked the bags in the cart and waited for Marcella. Eivind helped her pack her stuff up too, and we pushed the two carts out to the parking lot.

We requested two Ubers and loaded Marcella into one that would take her and all of my new stuff back to the marina. Eivind and I hailed another and went to a chandlery—a boat supply store.

Eivind helped me pick out a headlamp and a harness. Like a gentleman helping me with a jacket, Eivind held the harness up for me to stick my arms in.

"Now this strap"—he tugged at the webbing that dangled in front of my crotch—"goes like this." The strap slid through his fingers as the back of his hand swept down my shorts and stopped between my legs.

"Eivind!" I hissed at him.

"Yes?"

I looked around frantically. The shelves on either side of the aisle hid us from view, but enough people wandered the store to make me nervous.

Eivind's fingers pressed firmer, and for a millisecond I ground down against him. He smirked at me and kissed the corner of my mouth.

"Okay, really, Eivind." It came out breathier than I'd intended.

"Really?" he whispered.

I shook the spell off. "This is blatant misconduct, and as the personal safety officer tasked with keeping me alive, I expect more from you."

Eivind laughed. "Yes, ma'am." He tried to "help" me with the straps again and I pushed his hands away.

"I'm not falling for that," I muttered. Reaching in an awkward maneuver, I pushed the strap between my legs and grabbed it from behind. Eivind showed me how to clip it on the side of the harness.

"Well, that's bloody uncomfortable." I adjusted my shorts, which were giving me a front-wedgie. We fiddled with the straps until only half of my underwear was up my bum. Then Eivind moved on to the safety features.

A thick zipper ran from one side around my head to the other. Eivind pulled the zipper along and bright yellow material popped out.

"This is the inflating part." He dragged a matching fluorescent hood over my head. "Aw, you look so cute."

We also found a tether, and Eivind showed me how to clip it onto my harness. I'd use the other end to attach myself to the boat so I wouldn't fall off. Eivind said I didn't have to tether to the boat all the time, but I should use my tether if conditions were bad or if I was out on the deck.

I tried to pay, but Eivind insisted on using his card since the items would stay behind when I left.

When we returned to *Eik*, I sat down to bite the bullet. I called Dad at work first since he was an early riser and, frankly, the calmer of the two.

My mum did not take it well. She didn't yell at me, but she did that scary mum-silence before she answered.

"Honey, I need you to think about this. You don't know these people. What if I don't hear from you and you disappear? I don't know anything about them or where I would start to look for you!"

"I'll send you all the information you need, Mum. You'll have everyone's name and our contact information so you can email me while we are out at sea. Jonas has a cool tracker showing exactly where we are on the map."

"But what if something goes wrong? What if the boat sinks?"

I described all the safety supplies Jonas had on board, using my fancy new nautical words like *drogue* and *EPIRB*.

"I don't know about this, Lila. I don't trust strangers like this."

"But I do, Mum. Eivind will take good care of me." I looked up to find Eivind watching me, and smiled at him. Mum scoffed.

"You barely know him—"

I interrupted. "Mum, it's going to be okay. I'll email you every day. I promise."

Mum sighed. "I'm going to talk to your father when he comes home, and we will see about this."

I smiled a little bit. Dad would calm her down.

Twenty-Five

WE SAT AROUND THE TABLE EATING DINNER WHEN MY phone rang. Marcella had to let me out of the booth to grab it.

"Hi, Dad," I answered, heading up the companionway and into the cockpit for some privacy.

"Hey, sweet pea. Your mum is in a tizzy."

"Ugh. I know."

"If it would make your mum feel better, why don't you put Eivind on the phone to talk to me?"

"What? Dad! Absolutely not. You do not need to talk to Eivind. This is my decision!"

"Sweet pea, just let me talk to him."

I sighed and gripped my phone in my lap with both hands. Was it worth it to put my foot down? I decided not.

"Hey, Eivind?" I called down. "Could you come out here?"

People and plates shuffled around as Eivind made his way up to me.

"My dad wants to talk to you."

Eivind watched me for a moment and nodded. He took the phone from me and held it up to his ear. "Hallo?"

I strained to try to hear what Dad was saying, but he was too muffled for his words to make sense.

Eivind looked at me. "Yes, sir." He nodded. Eivind pulled the phone away from his ear and grabbed my hands with his. I realized I'd been wringing them. "Go downstairs, darling."

"But—"

He pulled me in and kissed my head. "It is fine. Go eat, okay?"

"Okay," I grumbled.

I sat back at the table with the rest of the crew and finished my dinner. By the time Eivind came back down, his food was cold. Marcella offered to reheat it, but Eivind said no and slid into the booth next to me. I passed his plate over and he gave me my phone back.

He took a bite and chewed, thinking for a moment. "Your dad is a little scary."

"What? No way! He's, like, a normal guy. He's not a cop or military or anything." I paused and fortified myself with some beer. "What did he say?"

"He asked if we were sleeping together."

"What? Oh my God, no. What did you say?"

"I told him the truth."

"WHAT? EIVIND."

Eivind started laughing.

"Are you serious?"

He laughed so hard he couldn't respond to me.

"Okay, you're kidding, very funny."

"I am not kidding." Eivind was still laughing, but he put his head in his hands. That was when I realized he was laughing hysterically . . . maybe even manically. "I told your dad we are sleeping together," he said with disbelief.

I gasped. "Oh my God, oh my God, oh my God."

Eivind ran his hands up over his head and then back down his face. "It is fine. He said he was glad I told him the truth." Eivind grinned at me and suddenly I was suspicious.

"What *exactly* did my dad say?"

"He said that he appreciated learning the truth from me directly instead of finding a used condom on your bedroom floor."

"Oh no." I groaned and put my head on the tabletop. Then I remembered that the rest of the crew was still in the salon, listening to our conversation. "I was a stupid, horny sixteen-year-old, okay? It was a rough patch with my dad, but I'm not anymore."

"Not horny anymore?" Eivind teased.

I shoved him with both hands, but he barely budged. "I'm not *stupid* anymore. Well. I'm less stupid, but that's all we can hope for anyway. What else did my dad say to you?"

Eivind's hand was warm on my skin as he rubbed my back. "He would fly anywhere in the world to help you if you needed it. And also fly anywhere in the world to cut my balls off if I hurt you."

"My dad said balls?"

"I am paraphrasing."

"If he hurts you," Marcella interrupted, "I'll knee him in the junk."

Elayna, who was using tongs to serve herself more salad, snapped them at Eivind's crotch with a menacing look.

"Whoa! Why the hate on my balls?" Eivind cupped them protectively.

My phone chimed.

I love you, sweet pea.

The next twenty-four hours were a blur of activity. Each of the crew members would randomly pop their heads in to give me some advice: *Lila, do you listen to podcasts? You should download some. Lila, did you buy enough shampoo? Lila, do you have enough clothes? You should buy a second bather.*

With Jonas, I also went over safety stuff. Jonas showed me their medical kit, which contained several different antibiotics, pain medication, and anti-nausea pills. We talked about emergencies, weather, and how the boat would be able to communicate with people onshore, which meant I could email my parents.

"Come here." Jonas crooked his finger, and I followed him to the desk. He pulled a slender book out of a plastic bag. The cover still had a price tag on it. "This is for you. It is more about the basics of sailing a small dinghy than a big oceangoing ship like *Eik*, but the principles are the same. You can learn the parts of the boat and some of the theory behind sailing, even more than you already know."

"Oh wow." I took the book and thumbed through it, looking at diagrams of little sailboats and wind vanes.

"Thank you! I am so excited to learn more, and I'll have plenty of time to read this underway."

I also had my e-reader heaped full with books, hundreds of hours of podcasts downloaded, and though Marcella and Elayna kept reminding me of things I might need, they also assured me that if I ran out of anything, I could use some of theirs.

Not having boat projects to do, I tried to keep to myself during the day. Eivind often worked on various projects, and he had me sit beside him while he worked. He called them "one-and-a-half-person jobs"—Eivind worked while I read next to him, and sometimes he would ask me to hand him a tool or flip a switch or dump some wash water overboard.

I voraciously read blogs about sailing while I still had access to the internet. The sailing itself would be boring, and I wondered if I had enough to occupy myself for twenty-five days. I was sure I had enough books and podcasts, but what if I tired of them?

It was five o'clock on our final night in Panama City. Marcella was slumped in the main salon, a damp cloth over her eyes. She'd spent the entire day organizing, cleaning, and reorganizing the galley.

Elayna stroked her hair. "What can I do to help?"

Marcella moaned. "I have to take one more trip to the store."

Elayna tsk-tsked. "Can I cook dinner while you do that?"

Eivind perked up. "I can make Spamaroni?"

"No!" Elayna and Marcella shouted together.

I giggled.

Peeking out from under the cloth, Marcella looked at Elayna. "There is lettuce and chicken for a salad. Can you just make a balsamic dressing?"

"Of course."

I stood up. "I'll help, and Eivind can drive you to shore."

Elayna and I busied ourselves around the galley, washing and chopping vegetables. Marcella would replace everything we used tonight with more fresh goods during her final trip to the supermarket. Her level of planning was epic. The fridge was stuffed full of fresh produce, and cans were stacked in every nook and cranny imaginable, not just in the galley, but under the floorboards and cushions. Sheets of paper were stacked up, her notes for meal planning: *Day 1 dinner: rice salad; Day 2 dinner: chicken curry.*

"Do you feel like you did everything you wanted to while you were here?" I asked Eivind when he returned.

"I mean, you were in Panama for what? A few days before I met you? You may have been in the country two weeks, but I don't think you explored much."

"You are right. I did not see much. It happens everywhere we go. Someone might fly to Panama City and spend two weeks and tour everything they wanted. For us a two-week visit is really only a few days. There is so much more we have to do to just live."

"Nah, yeah. I guess you all have been busy with provisioning and projects and paperwork. That's tough."

"It can be. But Jonas made the decision to sail quickly through the route he wanted to take. People circumnavigate the world in fifteen months or fifteen years."

"It's such a long time."

"Yes, but these people are still always moving. And maybe they spend a year or two here or there. But to Jonas, he wanted to be out here sailing. He likes the destinations, yes, but he likes the sailing more."

"What about you? Are you here for the places or the sailing?"

Eivind leaned on the counter, thinking. "I like sailing, but not enough to do many long passages. This much time at sea is hard, but shorter sailing trips are better. When we came through the Caribbean, that was ideal. Spend a few days or a week on one island, sail a few hours to the next one, and keep going. That was nice."

"Sailing more of a hobby, I guess?"

"Ja. A hobby."

"It's nice that you've stayed on to help, even if you don't like the long passages." I swept chopped tomatoes into a bowl. "What about you, Elayna?"

"I am in it for the sailing." She sighed. "I can't wait to be out at sea. Soon, Lila, you will see how remarkable it is."

Twenty-Six

THE NEXT MORNING WE ATE BREAKFAST TOGETHER. JONAS and Eivind went to shore to pay the marina bill and dispose of our trash. I sent one last email to my parents, and then I went out to the bow and took a selfie, the deck of *Eik* visible behind me. I started a new post:

I'm doing something a little crazy. Today I set sail to cross the Pacific Ocean with my new friends. As the sailors say, wish me "fair winds and following seas." I'll see you in twenty-five days!

When Eivind and Jonas returned, they put the dinghy back up on the davits, and Jonas quickly went over the departure checklist one last time. Every item was crossed off.

When everyone started putting their harnesses on, I put mine on too. All five of us stood on deck, and Jonas started up the engine. Eivind stood by the bow, and when Jonas gave him the okay, he untied the mooring line from the cleat.

Eik shifted away from the mooring, and Jonas pointed us out to sea.

We motored for a few minutes before Eivind and the rest of the crew started work on the sails. Jonas steered the boat into the wind and slowed us down. Though the waves didn't seem big, *Eik* bucked around. I gripped the metal rail of the cockpit, my stomach flipping—was it the motion of the boat and the waves tossing us about, or the fact that reality was hitting me and my decision was final? I really was sailing off into the Pacific Ocean.

The crew worked together to bring the mainsail up. When Eivind gave the signal, Jonas spun the wheel, turning *Eik* to port. We picked up speed, and there was this amazing moment of lift, like the boat was eager to take off and fly. The waves calmed, her bow steadied, and Jonas turned off the engine.

I closed my eyes, overwhelmed with the sensations. The crew still moved around me, but beyond that was the call of the ocean. The wind teased my hair, the waves caressed *Eik*'s hull, and the sun kissed my skin.

When I opened my eyes again, the genoa was unfurled and we'd picked up even more speed. Eivind coiled some lines next to me, tidying the boat up now that we were underway.

"Wow," I breathed.

Eivind crawled in to sit beside me. "Well, here we are! Sailing!"

Jonas grinned, pressed a few buttons, and slouched away from the helm.

We gathered back in the cockpit and Jonas went over a few things I didn't quite understand. He talked about the wind angle, the sail plan, the weather conditions . . . and my heart sank a little bit. I wondered if I might be in over my head. Eivind assured me that he'd help me when my shift started at noon.

Jonas wrapped up. "Eivind, I turn the helm over to you. Any questions?"

Eivind saluted Jonas and they switched positions so Eivind was by the helm. Jonas, Marcella, and Elayna all disappeared down below. Someone moved around in the galley.

"What should I do?" I asked Eivind.

"Whatever you want. I think maybe stay up here until you see how you feel with the seasickness."

Jonas's head popped out of the companionway and he handed Eivind his tablet. "Lila, do you need anything?"

"Can you grab my e-reader for me? It's on the table." Jonas reappeared with it a few moments later, and I settled into the corner of the cockpit.

I read a few chapters before my eyes tired. I closed them briefly, and the next thing I knew, Eivind was gently shaking me awake.

Groggily, I blinked up at him. "I guess I took a nap, huh?"

He smiled gently. "Yes, but that is good. It is almost time for your shift. Do you want anything to drink?"

"Is there some coffee?"

"Of course. I will be right back."

I eased myself up and looked around. There were some islands off in the distance, but they were hazy and behind us. I was the only one up top, and I could pretend I had the boat all to myself for a moment. How surreal it must be to sail alone.

Eivind came back up and my personalized briefing began.

"This box is the autopilot. Do not touch it. Because we have such a long way to go, the plan is to just set the sails right, set the autopilot, and let the boat do her thing.

Eivind pointed to big letters that spelled COG; this was followed by numbers: 187, 192, 189, 194 . . . the number kept changing. "This number here, this is our course over ground. We want it to be between 180 and 210. If it goes outside of that range, get Jonas. Next, look at this number." The letters read AWS. "Apparent wind speed. If this reads over fifteen, get Jonas. If you see something on the horizon, get Jonas. If you hear any weird noises—"

"Get Jonas?"

Eivind tweaked my nose. "Cheeky. Yes, get Jonas. But for today, I will be with you on watch, so you do not have to worry too much."

"Okay, the course over ground needs to be between 180 and 200?"

"Two hundred and ten."

"Two hundred and ten. Apparent wind speed is less than fifteen?"

"Yes."

"I need to write this down." I pulled my phone out and made a note.

"Most of the time," Eivind said, "you will do nothing. You can sit up here and read or whatever. Make sure every ten minutes you check the horizon around us. Look for anything new. That will be your whole watch."

"You make it sound so easy."

"It is. When everything is going right. When something goes wrong, that is when it is hard. But the rest of us are here to help you."

"Thank you."

"And do not leave the cockpit. Always wear your harness. Be safe, yes?"

"Yes." I nodded. "What's this thing here?" I pointed at a triangle on the screen.

"That is another boat." Eivind showed me how to pull up information on the boat. Through this system, we could learn the name, speed, destination, all kinds of interesting things.

"Here it says that we will pass twenty miles from this boat."

"Is that close enough to see?"

He shook his head. "Probably not. Maybe if it was a big cargo ship, but this one is a sailboat like us."

After a few more questions, Eivind settled in to play games on his tablet, and I had my e-reader, but it remained in my lap, untouched. Instead I sat still, quietly listening and looking around the boat.

Elayna came up and said lunch was ready. I stayed up top while Eivind made me a sanger—tuna salad. He brought it up for me to eat at the helm. A few minutes later he joined me and we shared a bag of chips.

I stayed alert the rest of my shift, and when it was done, Marcella came up to take over. We had our mini debriefing, led by Eivind, and I was off duty.

Plopping down next to Eivind, I snuggled up to him. He raised his arm to let me in closer, and I watched him move the cards around on his screen. He kissed my head. "We should go try to sleep."

"Yeah?"

"Sure. Sleep while we can. If you cannot sleep, just rest."

We moved down to our cabin, stripped off our clothes, and climbed into bed. I fell asleep instantly.

Twenty-Seven

EIVIND SHOOK ME AWAKE. THE CABIN WAS LIT WITH A golden light coming in from the edges of the swinging curtain.

"Dinner is ready."

Elayna ate up in the cockpit since she was on watch, but Eivind and I joined the rest of the crew in the main salon. Marcella served a cold rice salad. We ate quietly, everyone still waking up from their naps.

"Sunset time!" Elayna called down.

Eivind had explained that it was a ritual they kept on passage: dinner was served thirty minutes before sunset and then everyone sat out on deck to see the sun go down. It was one of the rare times the crew was all up and together while out at sea.

The sun slipped below the horizon, and I surveyed the ocean around us. We could no longer see land. There was nothing but the sea and the sky, three hundred and sixty degrees around us.

We stayed out on deck, watching the clouds bloom. When the colors peaked and started to darken, we trooped back downstairs. Eivind peeled off to go to sleep—his watch started at ten, so he hoped to sleep a few hours before then. Jonas was due to go on watch soon, and he spent some time downloading the weather. Marcella and I washed the small number of dishes from dinner.

I got the bowls clean, but my mind somersaulted—or was it my eyes? I stopped and bent over, leaning my head against the counter.

"Lila?"

"I'm okay. Just a little woozy."

Marcella patted my back. "You should go up top and look out at the horizon. That will help."

I stumbled toward the companionway and crawled up the stairs and onto the nearest cushion. I turned to look out over the water, and the fresh breeze on my face instantly brought my mind and stomach back into alignment. There was only a bare hint of sunset left. The moon was up and mostly full, casting enough light to illuminate everything around us. I laid my head down on my arm and looked at the moon sideways.

The fiberglass around me glowed red for a moment: Elayna's headlamp.

"Lila." She stroked my hair tenderly. "You aren't feeling well?"

I shrugged. Marcella came up the stairs behind me and the two women murmured together.

"Here," Elayna said. "Drink some water and eat some of these cookies."

I sat up a little and she handed me a cup of chilled water. I nibbled the cookies, and the ginger was sharp on my tongue.

"Tank oo," I said around a cookie.

"It's nothing."

I fell asleep while she stroked my hair.

———

I WOKE UP TO MORE MURMURING BEHIND ME. THIS TIME the two voices were male: Eivind and Jonas quietly doing the shift handover.

"Eivind?"

"Hey, darling. How are you feeling?"

I shoved some hair out of my face and turned over. He had his headlamp on and in his hand, the red light pointing down at the floor.

"Better."

"Ja? You ate some ginger cookies?"

"Yeah."

"Do you want some more?"

"No, I'm okay now."

"Do you want to stay up here or go to bed?"

I sat up further and looked around. *Eik* sailed along peacefully, and the moon approached the horizon. "I think I'll stay up here with you."

"Good. We put your headlamp over here." He pointed to a strap dangling out of a cup holder. "And this is your water. Can I check your harness?"

I sat up and let Eivind tug the straps and check the belts.

"Looks good. Come sit in the corner here with me. You can lean back here and look forward. That will help too."

Eivind and Jonas finished the handover, and I settled into the corner of the cockpit. I could stretch my legs out in front of me and, because the boat was slightly heeled over, I could see the horizon beyond the deck.

Jonas said good night and went down below with his stuff. Eivind came to sit next to me, where he could see the chartplotter comfortably. The smell of coffee, roasted dark, flowed over to me from his thermos.

We sat in silence for a while, our headlamps off. My eyes had adjusted to the night, and I could see surprisingly well over the boat. The moon cast sharp shadows against the deck.

I enjoyed the quiet, and Eivind did too, relaxing beside me. I let my mind wander, daydreaming a little, trying to imagine what the next few weeks would be like.

Eventually Eivind put one headphone in and music played quietly. I tilted my head back and gazed up at the stars, relaxing into the seat.

Eivind had woken me up at the end of his shift and guided me downstairs. I fell asleep quickly but had more trouble staying asleep this time. The noises of the sea and the boat kept jarring me awake.

Once, I had woken up in the pitch dark. Above me, something groaned and then stuttered, a sharp staccato noise.

"Eivind," I whispered. I poked his side and he grunted and rolled toward me. "What's that noise?"

He blinked a few times and listened, but all was quiet. He yawned. "I do not know. But you have to trust your crew. If there is a problem and they need us, they will wake us up."

He slipped quickly back to sleep. I lay awake, listening to someone take steps around the cockpit and make more noises, but I must have fallen asleep again; when I rolled over next, Eivind was gone.

I tried to motivate myself to rise for breakfast. The boat rocked as we sailed along and voices came from the salon. Eivind was out there, possibly on watch again.

What finally chased me out of bed was my wicked morning breath. As lazy as I felt, I could not go another minute without remedying the situation.

Dressing quickly, I stumbled out of our room and found Jonas on his laptop and Marcella in the galley. Marcella immediately poured a thermos of coffee for me.

"Thank you." I sipped and, finding the temperature just right, gulped in a mouthful and swished it around.

I looked up to find Jonas staring at me.

I shrugged. "Morning breath's best cure is coffee. How are we doing?" I leaned over the table to look at his screen, where he had a chart open. I could see a little boat icon; I presumed that was where we were.

"We are doing good, sailing well so far. The wind is supposed to shift this afternoon, maybe during your watch."

I hummed and nodded. After putting my harness on, I climbed up the companionway. Marcella kindly handed me my thermos again.

"Hey, darling," Eivind said. He was drinking coffee too and tilted his head up for a kiss. I leaned down and pressed my lips to his, and then settled into the corner again.

The day was bright, with a few clouds on the horizon. "How is your watch?" I asked.

"Good. I have not touched the sails. I did see a few boats, though. Still plenty of activity out here."

I studied the chartplotter more, and Eivind named everything I pointed to. The screen was full of acronyms: SOG, TWD, DTW. Eivind explained all of them, and I worked hard to remember each one, but I knew I was going to have to ask again and again.

We transitioned into my watch.

"Same instructions as yesterday," Eivind said while I ate a sanger at the helm.

"Fifteen AWS, 180 to 210 COG!"

Eivind saluted me and slumped onto the bench. He closed his eyes and leaned his head back.

"Are you okay?" I asked.

He nodded. "The second day is the worst. I am very tired because I do not sleep well the first night. It gets better after this."

"You should go down below and sleep. I'll join you at the end of my shift."

He cracked an eye open. "You will be okay, yes?"

I gave him a thumbs-up, and the corners of his mouth lifted. He hauled himself to his feet, kissed my head, and shuffled down the stairs.

I was entirely alone. Everyone on the boat was downstairs sleeping, trusting me with their lives. My heart raced, the weight of responsibility on me, and I wondered briefly if they were all idiots for leaving me in charge.

But I remembered that Jonas did this all the time, leaving his boat, his home, in someone else's hands. The sky was clear and the weather fair. We'd coasted along for an entire day already without much fanfare.

Relaxing back into my seat, I kept an eye on the horizon and on my numbers as the waves flew by.

All too quickly, Marcella's head came into view from the salon.

"Buongiorno!"

"Hello!" I called back. "How was your nap?"

Marcella slumped down next to me. "Wonderful. How are things up here?" Before I could respond, she leaned forward, eyes roaming over the chartplotter. "Yes, this is good." She poked her head out the side of the cockpit and looked up at the sails. "Everything looks good, yes?"

"I think so."

"Good job. I am proud of you." She hugged my shoulders. "No other boats or anything?"

I shook my head.

"Then I will take over from here. Have a good nap."

Saluting sloppily, I left the cockpit and carefully climbed down the stairs. Disentangling myself from my harness, I brushed my teeth before I slipped into bed next to Eivind, who didn't wake but curled his arms around me.

Twenty-Eight

I WOKE UP TO MOVEMENT UNDER MY FACE. I BLINKED MY eyes open and tried to process what was going on. Eivind's chest was under my cheek, his T-shirt rubbing against my skin while he fidgeted.

I moved a little bit and then felt it: Eivind's T-shirt was wet. I brought my hand up and tilted my head to look at his shirt. I sat bolt upright.

"What the hell?"

"Umm . . ." Eivind was at a loss for words.

"Eivind," I said. "Did I *drool* on you? Oh my God, I did. Eivind, that's a puddle of drool on your shirt! I am so sorry—I have never done that before. I swear, that doesn't normally happen."

Eivind started laughing, and I punched him *mildly hard* in his ribs. He let out an *oof*, but didn't stop giggling. I punched him again.

"Okay, okay! It is okay, Lila. It happens." He wiped tears from his eyes and sat up. Grabbing the hem of his shirt, he pulled it away from his skin to look at the huge splotch of dampness.

"Oh my God." I covered my head in my hands. How gross. How mortifying.

"Lila," he said. "This happens to people who are a little seasick. Your body produces more"—he gestured to his mouth—"what did you call it? Drool?"

"Seriously? That happens? Why on *earth* does my mouth think it's okay to drool when I'm seasick? What fucking purpose does that serve?"

Eivind shrugged and reached back to tug his shirt over his head. He inspected his chest before wiping it off with his shirt.

I died of mortification and face-planted back onto the bed.

The mattress around me dipped and Eivind waited above me. He trailed kisses up my spine, pressing his lips to the fabric of my tank top, and I shuddered when they passed over the edge and onto my bare skin. He nipped my shoulder, teased my neck, and gently stroked his lips over the shell of my ear. Despite my humiliation, I arched my back, pressing up into his body.

He inhaled and gently whispered, "Watch out for soggy pillows."

I chased him out of the room with my—*dry*—pillow.

I WENT INTO THE GALLEY, WIPING SLEEP FROM MY EYES and yawning. Marcella and Elayna worked in the kitchen, frying bread and dicing fruit. The boat always smelled like the big boule loaves that Marcella baked at least once a day to feed the five of us. Onshore, it was faster and easier to buy a loaf from the store, but bread bought on land would take up too much space and wouldn't last long.

"Toast, Lila?" Elayna asked.

"Yes, please." I sat on the couch next to Eivind and stole his mug of coffee.

"Woman!" he protested. I smirked and offered him my lips as a condolence prize and he swept a kiss into my mouth.

Until Elayna whacked me with a kitchen towel.

"We might have to ban PDA from the salon." She handed Eivind a new mug of coffee and set a plate down in front of me.

On the table was a collection of spreads and a platter of cheese and meats sitting on a foam pad. I picked through the jars, looking at my choices: marmalade, butter, honey . . .

"Oh, I bought something for breakfast! I'll be right back." I went into our cabin and dug around until I found my Aussie treat—Vegemite.

"What is that?" Eivind asked when I returned to the table.

"Vegemite. Have you ever had it before?"

"I have heard of it." Eivind made to open the lid. "Can I?"

I nodded and he twisted the lid off and took a whiff. He immediately jerked his head away in disgust.

"What the hell is this?"

"Rude. Give it back, you heathen."

"You are going to eat that?"

"Yes! It's delicious."

Marcella and Elayna came to the table with their plates and sat down. Marcella snickered when Elayna lifted the jar to her nose and cautiously sniffed.

I ignored them and grabbed the butter, slathering it on my toast while the bread was still warm. Eivind watched with fascination while I spread a thin layer of Vegemite over the butter.

237

"That is so little Vegemite." He pinched his thumb and forefinger together. "What is the point?"

"It's strong—you have to have the right bread-to-butter-to-Vegemite ratio," I explained. I took a satisfying bite out of my slice and rolled my eyes back. "Ugh, it's so good."

Eivind's eyes locked onto my mouth and his tongue darted out to lick his lips. I moaned again and his eyes flared.

Jonas didn't even look up from his laptop. "I will hose you off if I have to."

Eivind grinned.

"Wanna try it?"

He tentatively took a bite and chewed. He looked thoughtful, a sommelier tasting the hottest new vintage. Swallowing, he brought his coffee up and took a few large gulps.

"Disgusting," he confirmed.

"You eat pickled herring."

He shrugged. "I like lutefisk better."

"What's that?"

He grinned at me. "Dried fish with salt . . . pickled in . . ."

"Lye," Marcella supplied.

He nodded. "Lye."

I grimaced and offered the Vegemite around the table, but no one else wanted a bite.

"I've had it before," Marcella said. "No, thank you."

Fine, this jar of Vegemite was all mine.

Twenty-Nine

WHILE NAPPING, I AWOKE TO A KNOCK ON OUR DOOR. Eivind and I were both in bed, clothed and sleeping, so he lifted his head and said to come in.

The door opened enough for Elayna's head to fit through. "It is almost time to do the equator crossing!"

"Okay, we will be up in a few minutes."

For hundreds of years, sailors have held ceremonies as they crossed the equator, and it was our turn. We were "pollywogs," the uninitiated bottom-of-the-barrel crew, hoping to cross the equator with a blessing from King Neptune and earn our new title of "shellback."

The crew had warned me about it before we left Panama, and I'd researched the tradition, my eyes growing with the crazy stories of sailors being dunked in rotten kitchen scraps or forced to drink beer until they puked, but Eivind had assured me that our equator crossing was strictly fun—a talent show and playtime.

Eivind and I dressed in our bathers and came outside, where we helped Elayna and Marcella bring the sails in. First, they furled in the genoa sail in the front, then brought the boat into the wind and dropped the mainsail. Eivind pulled out a little bit of the genoa sail again, "to keep us on course," he said.

We inched our way toward the equator. The chartplotter, in the upper right-hand corner of the screen, had our exact coordinates, and we estimated we had about twenty minutes to go.

A laugh burst out of me when Jonas came up the stairs in full King Neptune attire: a bedsheet toga was slung over one shoulder, an aluminum foil crown was on his head, and a great big bushy fake beard was strapped to his chin. In one hand he held a makeshift trident, made from a boat hook and some cardboard; in his other hand he'd created a scroll out of two paper towel rolls. I couldn't stop grinning at the normally serious Jonas going through all this effort to make today special for us.

He dropped one of the cardboard tubes and the scroll unfurled, revealing printer paper taped together, making the scroll a meter long. In a deep, booming voice, inexplicably tinged with a British accent, Jonas read:

"Hear ye, hear ye, hear ye. I am King Neptune's representative, sent to escort the ship *Eik* on its journey from the northern hemisphere to the southern hemisphere. King Neptune demands a sacrifice to be made for safe passage across the equator. Who dares to go first?"

Eivind stepped forward and saluted King Neptune. "I am First Mate Eivind."

I grabbed an invisible skirt hem and curtsied. "I am Lila, a hitchhiker."

"A hitchhiker? How rebellious of you. Very well, I shall hear you plead your case."

Eivind sat in the corner of the cockpit bench and I sat behind him on the backrest. He strummed his ukulele a few times before breaking into the opening bars of "Over the Rainbow." I joined in singing—I'm not very good, but I kept up with it and Eivind sang the melody, complementing my voice.

When we were done, the rest of the crew applauded, and we bowed for our audience.

"Very good," said King Neptune. "Who is next?"

Elayna stepped forward. "I am Elayna, a deckhand aboard *Eik*." She reached into the bag by her side and pulled out three oranges. "I will juggle for my passage."

While we weren't moving quickly, *Eik* did bob and sway in the waves and I watched in disbelief as Elayna started to juggle the three oranges. She planted her feet wide in the cockpit at the helm and tossed each orange up. As the boat moved, she swayed her hips or bent her knees, gimballing her body to stay level.

With each trick, we gasped and clapped until one particularly bad lurch knocked the oranges off balance enough that they tumbled to the floor around the cockpit. We all scrambled after them, laughing and attempting to catch them before they went overboard.

"Nicely done, nicely done." King Neptune applauded. He turned to Marcella. "And what do you have to present to appease King Neptune?"

Marcella saluted. "I am Marcella, galley wench extraordinaire. And I have a special treat for King Neptune—and the crew!"

Marcella disappeared downstairs and returned with a plate full of mini tarts. Each tart was delicately swirled with whipped cream, and as I bit into mine, the sweetness of the chocolate mousse inside hit my tongue.

Everyone made appreciative yummy noises while we ate our bite-sized treats. Jonas—I mean King Neptune—ate the last one. Then he swallowed and wiped his hands off.

"I am pleased to announce that King Neptune has deemed you all worthy pollywogs and has granted you permission to sail over the equator and into the southern hemisphere."

We all cheered, "Huzzah, King Neptune! *Bravissimo!*" and Eivind wolf-whistled loudly.

Jonas turned to Marcella. "King Neptune declares that some libations are in order."

Marcella disappeared downstairs again and handed us our plastic wineglasses and a chilled bottle of sparkling wine. King Neptune poured us each a glass.

Eivind climbed out to the back of the boat with the bottle of wine and, holding his glass in one hand and the bottle in the other, tipped the bottle to spill some wine overboard, a tithing to King Neptune. We raised our glasses in a toast.

"To crossing the equator!"

We drank and laughed, teasing one another over our talent shows. Elayna told us she had picked up juggling from a man she'd hooked up with once in the

Mediterranean—he had been an entertainer on a cruise ship.

"Okay, it is hot under this toga." Jonas broke character and stripped his toga and beard off. He sat at the helm, keeping an eye on the chartplotter. After a few minutes, he downed the last of his drink, climbed to the back of the boat, and lowered the swim ladder down.

"Is it really safe for all of us to go swimming?" I asked.

"We are going to set up a line," Jonas answered, "floating from one side of the boat to another, a big loop. We will swim near the loop. With the sails down and no wind, *Eik* will be gently bobbing along."

He pulled a line out of one of the cubbies in the cockpit and went to work setting it up. When both ends were tied to the boat, he tossed it overboard.

"Roll the sail in."

Eivind cranked down on the winch and the genoa furled up. *Eik* slowed.

"Just a few moments left!" Jonas called out. "Three . . . two . . . one!" He pulled out a bullhorn and blew it. Eivind hooted and leaped off the back into the water. He splashed and resurfaced, howling.

Jonas rolled his eyes. "Your swimming pool, ladies."

I let Marcella and Elayna stand on the edge first. They both leaped into the air together and squealed as they splashed around. I eyed the ocean carefully as I stepped down onto the swim platform. The water was so clear, I could see everyone's legs kicking, keeping them on the surface. Eivind was further out, toward the loop, but he dove down and kicked, propelling himself back to the stern.

"Oh, Jesus," I muttered under my breath.

"Darling." Eivind chuckled. "Are you scared?"

"Okay, it's unreasonable. I *know* that the boat is not going to float away and I'm not going to drown and nothing is going to eat me. But it's still scary."

"Do you want a snorkel mask?" Jonas offered from above me. "Maybe it will help you to put your face under the water and look down."

"No, I can do this."

"Do you want to jump together?" Eivind called up.

I considered. "Yeah, okay."

"Okay." He climbed out of the water and offered me his hand. I gripped it tightly in mine. "On the count of three. One. Two. Three!"

Eivind and I leaped off the step and out into the Pacific Ocean. We both splashed under and resurfaced, hair slicked onto our faces, laughing at the cool slide of water on our skin.

"Do you want to hold on to me?"

I nodded and he welcomed me in for a water-treading snuggle. I wrapped my arms and legs around him and he kicked hard, keeping us afloat.

"It scares me more than I thought it would. It's so endlessly deep. Like looking out into space or something."

"I am proud of you." Eivind kissed my cheek and I grinned at him.

Jonas threw some toys out: a few pool noodles, a beach ball, and, at my request, a snorkel mask. I disengaged from Eivind and donned the mask.

I put my face below the surface of the water and looked down into the abyss. The water was blue, blue, blue, with beams of light streaming down from the surface.

To my right was *Eik*, floating peacefully in the water. I could see her bottom! Thanks to my little sailing book, I could identify the keel, a heavy flange in the middle of the hull balancing the boat upright, and the rudder, a rotating board at the stern we used to steer.

We splashed around in the water until we grew tired or cold. When Eivind climbed out, Jonas hopped in, putting a mask and weight belt on, free diving down to inspect the underwater parts of the boat.

There was a hose in the cockpit that provided fresh water for us to shower with. We took turns rinsing the salt off our skin and toweling ourselves dry, sharing two beach towels between the four of us.

"This is a big bruise." Eivind traced a finger gently over a blue-and-purple spot on my thigh.

"I know. I think I ran into the kitchen counter? I have another one here." I pointed at my shin.

Eik moved constantly under my feet, making it hard to stay balanced, and I often walked around like a drunken sailor.

"I have a few too." Marcella twisted her arm around so I could see a fading yellow spot on the back. "We call them boat bites. For when *Eik* jumps up and gets you."

"Boat bites. I love it."

When Jonas climbed on board, he and Elayna began to set the sails again, *Eik* picking up speed and back on course. Marcella began preparing dinner, and Eivind and I slid back downstairs for a rest. We fell asleep quickly, rocked by the boat and tired from our biggest adventure in days.

After dinner, we watched the sunset together. Jonas came up last, carrying a stack of papers.

"I have something for you all." He looked down and read from the top paper. "Marcella." He handed it to her. "Lila. Elayna."

The paper was burnt at the edges, with tea stains and soot smudges. I read the print:

I, Captain Jonas, declare that Lila Ryan has crossed the equator aboard the good ship Eik. *She has been declared worthy by King Neptune, and a capable crew member by her captain.*

00°00.000 North, 088°54.484 West

Jonas had signed his name below it as the captain, and *Eik*'s official stamp sealed it. Opposite, a line was indicated for King Neptune, and a stylized wave served as the signature.

It brought tears to my eyes. Looking up, the rest of the crew was misty-eyed as well.

Jonas and Eivind embraced, muttered Norwegian passing between them. Pulling back, they smiled at each other and clapped shoulders.

With a glance at Elayna and Marcella, the three of us crowded in and gave Jonas a group hug. He laughed and hugged us back.

Downstairs, Eivind brought some tape into our cabin and posted our certificates on the wall. Stepping back, we both admired them.

I intertwined my fingers with Eivind's. "You have a good brother."

Thirty

THE NEXT AFTERNOON, I WOKE UP FROM MY SECOND NAP of the day to find Eivind reading next to me in bed. I quickly checked the pillow under my face for drool—it was dry—and sat up.

"What time is it?"

Eivind rolled over and glanced at his phone. "Four forty-five. We still have a few hours before dinner."

I grunted and buried my face back into my pillow. Eivind chuckled and resumed reading, but a few minutes later I rolled over and grabbed my e-reader too. I snuggled into Eivind's body and he wrapped an arm around me.

"No more sleeping?"

"Yeah, nah. I'm awake. I'll see how it feels reading for a little bit."

We read quietly together for a few minutes, but then Eivind put his book down. His fingers came up and stroked my hair while I read. He rolled into me a little and kissed my forehead, my temple, and down to my ear.

"How do you feel?" he whispered.

I smiled. "Not as good as you, but I like where this is going."

Eivind plucked my e-reader from between us and set it down behind him. When he returned, he cupped my jaw with his hand, tilting my face up. His lips coaxed mine open for a deep, sweeping kiss, and we both inhaled.

"If you feel too seasick, tell me, yes?"

I nodded and pulled him back down to my mouth. Eivind rolled over me, his hands pushing up my tank top and wedging between my back and the bed.

We kissed and panted, grinding together through our clothes, trying to find an impossible rhythm while the boat moved around under us. Eivind was patient, but his body strained harder the longer we went.

I pushed him off me and began to undress: no finesse, no teasing. Thankfully, Eivind stripped too, and we tumbled back into bed together.

My head rested on his forearm; his legs tangled with mine. Eivind's hard cock rested against my hip, a touch of dampness on my skin while his fingers trailed over my torso.

His hand slid between my legs and he groaned at the wetness he found there. Teasing me, he used a gentle touch and I gasped, pulling away to breathe. Eivind moved to kiss down my neck, then gently sucked on my shoulder.

His fingers slid around me and into me over and over again, and my body strained, pinned down beneath his hips.

Finally I begged, "Please!"

"Show me exactly how you like it," he rasped in my ear.

I put his finger to the perfect spot and applied just the right pressure. A few strokes and I cried out, coming underneath him.

Cool air touched my skin where Eivind had been. I turned my head to watch him roll on a condom and he crawled back onto the bed, kneeling between my legs. He put a hand on my thigh, pushing my leg up. I moved my other leg up too, opening myself further. Eivind guided himself in and pressed deep, his eyes clenched shut in pleasure.

He gripped both of my thighs, spreading my legs wide and pushing my knees closer to my chest. Tilting his head, he gazed down as he delivered a slow stroke in and out of my body.

He did it again, and I watched his abs as he rolled his hips, the muscles contracting and releasing.

I reached for a pillow and pulled it down, using it to prop up my head so I could watch Eivind better. I tilted my hips a bit more, and I could fully see our bodies joining.

Eivind shifted to give himself a better angle and grip and he started stroking, building up a rhythm. With every press, I wiggled a little further up the bed, until Eivind had to adjust again. He pulled out, pressed his hands on my butt cheeks, and pushed me all the way up the bed.

"Hands on the wall," he commanded.

I pressed my palms into the wall as Eivind pushed back in. With us working together, he thrust harder, building us both up. Eivind squeezed the back of my thighs with his hands.

"Lila," he panted. "Can you come again?"

I repositioned and used one hand on myself. Eivind swore, his eyes round and dilated, watching me touch myself. He kept up the pace, driving me steadily toward climax.

"Fuck! Lila, hurry!" he pleaded.

Our eyes connected and a few seconds later my body curved up and clenched around him, my knees trying to squeeze together, and I whimpered into my orgasm.

Eivind ground into my hips and came. He twitched and shuddered, his hands squeezing me to the point of pain.

Finally we both collapsed, Eivind's weight pressing me against the bed, our breath coming out ragged in each other's ear. He lay limp for a moment but then tried to push himself up. I wrapped my legs around him before he could pull out, and I tugged him back down above me. He huffed a laugh into my neck but settled against me.

I savored every inch of my sweaty skin rubbing his. I closed my eyes and leaned my head against him, working to catch my breath. My fingernails ran over his head, massaging his scalp.

When Eivind was in danger of slipping out, he pulled back and away, taking care of the condom. We both used the head and cleaned up before returning to lounge nude in bed. I dozed off and on, Eivind reading beside me until the knock sounded for dinner.

When it was time for Eivind's night watch, we strapped on our harnesses and went upstairs. I sat in the corner while Jonas briefed Eivind, and said good night as the captain went downstairs.

Eivind fiddled around for a few minutes at the helm. I read in the corner, and we settled into the quiet. Since my seasickness had disappeared, I'd been spending most of my time reading, finishing a book or two a day.

"Lila," Eivind said, interrupting my reading. "I have a surprise for you."

"Yeah?" I perked up. "What's my surprise?"

"Follow me." Eivind grabbed two pillows and climbed over the bench seats to the back of the boat. *Eik* had a wide-open space on the back, and we clipped our tethers in and lay down on the deck, pillows under our heads.

"Holy shit."

Eivind chuckled next to me and grabbed my hand. "The moon has been up on my shift so far. Tonight it has set already."

Stretched up over us were thousands of stars. More stars than I had ever seen in my life, from horizon to horizon.

"Look over there." Eivind pointed to my right.

I squinted. "What is that? A cloud?"

"No. It is the Milky Way."

We stayed on deck for the rest of the shift. Eivind played around with a stargazing app on his phone, pointing out constellations and naming stars. I spotted a shooting star out of the corner of my eye—a flash so bright but so quick.

After Marcella took over the watch, I reluctantly went inside, and we got ready for bed. Eivind fell asleep quickly, and I watched him, pondering all the parts of the world he could show me.

Thirty-One

I woke up to footsteps and shouting above me. At the foot of the bed, Eivind struggled to throw clothes on in his excitement.

"What's going on?"

"The fishing rod is going off!"

I listened carefully and heard a high-pitched whirring coming from the stern. Eivind left the room and hurried to the cockpit while I got out of bed and dressed. A few days ago, Eivind and Jonas had begun putting the fishing lines out first thing in the morning and, after sunset every night, reeling them back in.

Upstairs, I found the whole crew on deck. Jonas held the fishing pole and cranked the reel with one hand. The tip of the rod curved down toward the water and Jonas struggled.

With a surge, the line started to feed out a little bit, the reel clicking.

"No, no, no, no." Jonas muttered. He turned a knob on the side of the reel.

"Not too tight!" Eivind said.

"Ja, ja."

Eivind bounced on his toes, cheering his brother on. Jonas fought and broke out in a sweat.

"Do you want me to take a turn?" Eivind asked.

"Nei," Jonas grunted, never taking his eyes off the rod.

As it pulled closer, we could see it on the surface: a flash of silver and yellow swimming behind us.

And then the fish darted down. I couldn't see it anymore. The tip of the rod bent further, and Elayna gasped behind me.

"No!" Eivind howled. "Come back here, you fucker!"

Jonas just gritted his teeth. His persistence paid off: soon the fish was at the surface again, this time close enough to grab.

Eivind retrieved a gaff from one of the lockers. Marcella laid a tarp over the back deck and had a sheathed filet knife nearby.

Leaning out, Eivind grasped the line with a gloved hand and swung the hook. I couldn't see what happened, but it must have been a hit. Eivind let go of the line, grabbed the gaff with both hands, and heaved hard.

The fish that came up was bigger than I'd expected. At half Eivind's length, it was thick in the middle and the top was a dark blue while the bottom half was silver. Its eyes rolled around, tail slapping the air in its panic.

Eivind quickly laid it down on the tarp and pinned it with his knee. Marcella came in and slit the fish's underside crosswise from gill to gill. Blood poured out and the fish twitched, then went still.

I couldn't help but smile at our fortune from the sea. Everyone else grinned too, the excitement palpable. But Eivind didn't move as he watched the fish bleed out. Then I found out why—the fish went into death throes, the body spasming violently against the deck, Eivind holding on throughout the thrashing.

Finally the fish lay dead and Eivind removed himself. He and Jonas worked together to tie a line around its tail, its firm fins acting as a handle, and hoisted it overboard.

"What are you doing?" I asked.

"Bleeding the fish," Eivind said. "It makes the meat taste better."

Marcella and Elayna worked to rinse the blood off the tarp and the brothers high-fived.

"Wow," Jonas said. "That was a fight."

"That is the biggest fish we've caught," Eivind agreed.

"For sure. It's a yellowfin tuna. It is going to be so good," Marcella exclaimed.

I leaned over the lifeline to look at our catch. The head was occasionally dunked, the salt water washing off the blood.

It dragged over the side for a few minutes, then Jonas hoisted it onto the deck again—"Do not want to attract too many sharks and lose our catch"—and Marcella went to work.

Lightly running my fingers down the skin of the fish, I found that it was soft, like stroking the smoothest leather.

"It's beautiful," I said. "Makes me a little sad, actually." I frowned, thinking about the life we'd taken now that the excitement was over.

"It is a little sad." Jonas crouched down next to me. "But I think about the other meat we eat: the chickens, pigs, cows who have all had horrible lives. Or the fish in the supermarket, raised in a fish farm with runoff, or caught in a net with turtles, dolphins, and other life." He patted the body beneath us. "This fish, it had a great, wild life. It was a quick death, and we will not let it be wasted."

I nodded, blinking away tears. "That's a beautiful way to look at it, Jonas."

Marcella hunched over the fish, sawing away. The knife was sharp, but it was backbreaking work. Elayna helped, bringing up a platter for the loins Marcella cut from the carcass.

It took longer to cut the fish up than it did to catch it, but in the end, Marcella had four tuna loins, the meat shiny and strawberry red.

"How much meat do you think that is?" Eivind asked her.

She wiped the sweat off her brow with her forearm before replying. "Maybe ten servings per loin, four loins, eight meals?"

Downstairs, Marcella prepared the meat for freezing and shoved as much of it as she could into the freezer. We didn't have room for all of it, so the rest went into the fridge.

"Tuna for breakfast, lunch, and dinner," she teased.

"LUNCH TODAY IS TUNA POKE. THIS IS THE LAST OF IT."

We'd been eating tuna at every meal since we'd caught it several days prior. Marcella mixed the menu up, making sushi rolls one day, seared tuna another. She had to be creative with serving the same thing for days on end.

"Yum. What do we have for the condiments?" Eivind gestured at the various bowls and jars open on the tabletop.

Marcella pointed out each one. "Soy sauce, pickled ginger, here are some quick-pickled cucumbers and onions I made, brown rice . . ."

I started scooping items into my bowl, adding some wasabi and carrots, secretly wishing for some edamame to go with it.

"I looked at the weather forecast," Jonas said over the cacophony of noises as everyone made their plates. "The wind is dying, and should stay pretty low over the next few days."

Eivind perked up. "Does that mean we should get the spinnaker out after lunch?"

Thanks to my sailing book, I knew that spinnakers were very big sails made of thin material that could be used when the wind was really light.

"Ja. It is a good day for it. We can get it up this afternoon and then take it down before sunset."

"We don't leave it up all night?" I asked.

Eivind shook his head. "It is too dangerous. If a storm came up and we had to take it down quickly, we would need several people, and the risk of losing someone overboard would be too high. So we will only use it during the day."

"You know, I could start taking a night shift now. I'm comfortable during the day watches, and I'm sleeping well and not seasick anymore."

Jonas shrugged. "We are set in our schedules now—there is no need to change them."

We ate quickly, and then the rest of the crew got to work. I stayed out of the way as they ran around the deck, positioning the lines just so. Finally, from the helm, Jonas used a crank to raise up something called a sock, which bundled the sail up. As he hauled it up, the sail filled with wind and *Eik* flew.

Jonas sat back and wiped the sweat off his brow. The huge crimson sail led the way, a startling color against the blue sky and sea around us.

"What is our speed now?" Jonas asked me as Eivind and Elayna climbed back into the cockpit.

I checked the screen. "Eight-point-one, eight-point-three . . ."

"She looks very good." Eivind wrapped an arm around his brother's shoulders as *Eik* cut through the water.

———————

OUR ROUTINE WAS FAIRLY STABLE NOW, AND I SLEPT WELL enough that I woke up with Eivind and we did his morning shift together.

I climbed up the cockpit stairs to look for Jonas. He sat at the back of the cockpit, sipping a hot drink—decaf tea, probably—and gazing out at the ocean. The look on his face was so peaceful and serene, I hated to disturb him.

He turned and spotted me anyway.

"Morning."

He smiled and tipped his drink to me, shifting in his seat and dropping his feet to the deck. I took the corner opposite him.

"You look so peaceful out here."

"I love sunrise. Sunset is nice to enjoy with the crew, but I have the schedule that gives me sunrise all to myself. It is a beautiful way to start the day."

Eivind appeared at the companionway and handed me my coffee.

"Yeah, nah, I like a leisurely morning in bed."

The two brothers went over the conditions and sail plan, and once Eivind and I were settled in, Jonas disappeared down below.

I sipped my coffee while I watched Eivind in his deck harness and shorts. He checked the chartplotter and horizon, then walked the deck, checking lines and rigging. Then he stood in the cockpit, facing forward, and started squatting down and getting back up, squatting down and getting back up.

"What are you doing?" I giggled.

He looked at me over his shoulder. "Exercising."

He did more squats, and I tilted my head, watching his butt flex and tighten.

"Do you do this every morning?"

"It helps me wake up."

I ran a hand over my face. "God, you're exhausting." Though I had to admit, I didn't mind the view.

Eivind did squats, push-ups, sit-ups, jumping jacks, and more until he was sweating. The movements were challenged by *Eik*, who did her best to knock Eivind off his feet. Several times he tipped over onto the bench and had to right himself.

"Is *Eik* biting you?" I asked after a particularly bad lurch had Eivind rubbing his knee.

"Maybe you should be doing some of these. It helps get energy out."

"I have all the energy I need for reading, thank you very much."

"Marcella and Elayna do yoga sometimes."

I blanched. "On a moving boat? How is that even possible?"

Eivind showed off by moving into downward dog.

"You tosser." I threw a pillow at him.

Thirty-Two

A KNOCK CAME ON OUR CABIN DOOR. THROUGH HALF-lidded eyes crusted with sleep, Eivind and I looked at each other and tugged the sheet up over our naked bodies.

"Yeah?" he said in a sleep-weary voice. Guessing by the light coming through the window, it was mid-morning and we were in the middle of our sleep time.

The door opened and Jonas poked his head into the cabin. "I'm going to need some help. We have a problem with one of the lines."

"Ja," Eivind replied, and Jonas ducked out of the room.

Eivind swung his legs out of bed and dressed. I followed, albeit at a slower pace. When I came up into the cockpit, with my harness strapped on, Elayna was still up and Jonas explained the issue.

"Elayna woke me up early. She was walking on the deck and tossing a flying fish overboard when she noticed the tack line for the spinnaker is chafing at the block. We need to bring the sail down and replace the line."

Eivind nodded, and they discussed which line to use for the replacement. I knew from my book on sailing basics that the tack line was one of the three lines holding the sail onto the boat: the tack line was the bottom, the halyard was the top, and the sheet was the third line in the middle.

I stood out of the way while Jonas and Eivind prepared to furl the sail, putting lines on winches and bringing the spinnaker pole down.

Jonas started to crank the furling line in, twisting the drum at the bottom of the sail. Eivind released the sheet, allowing the sail to wrap tightly around the leading edge while Elayna waited at the tack with the replacement line.

I carefully maneuvered out to the middle of the deck, where I could lean against the mast and watch everyone work.

Suddenly there was a *thunk* and Elayna called to Jonas, "Stop! Stop!"

She crouched down at the base of the sail, inspecting the hardware and line. Jonas waited at the winch.

"Jonas! We have a problem!" Elayna shouted back at him.

He quickly wove through the rigging and bent down next to Elayna. When he saw the problem, his eyes widened.

"Give me the line," he said urgently.

I felt so powerless. I didn't understand what was happening, and even if I did, I would be no help.

Jonas quickly tied the line to the base of the furling drum and, rushing, threaded the line through the deck hardware and cleated it off. No sooner had he finished then the block at the base of the tack line exploded and the line holding the sail down to the deck snapped. I gasped as Elayna and Jonas both stumbled backward and struggled to regain their balance.

The force of the sail and the wind flung the furling drum out toward the sea, but it was stopped by the new line Jonas had just put on. The whole boat shuddered and careened for a moment before righting itself. The sail was still up and full, but flying off the side of the boat instead of the bow.

My eyes round, I looked back at Eivind. His eyes were wide too, his mouth open in shock. I didn't know much about sailing, but I knew how fortunate we were that Jonas had gotten the line down in time.

Eivind ran his hands over his head and bent down. "Fuck!"

Marcella was behind him, face grim.

"Okay, back to the cockpit, everyone," Jonas commanded. The five of us gathered around the helm. "The sail is fine for a few minutes, but we do need to get it down. Without the furler, this is going to be hard. We are going to have to drop the halyard down and pull the sail in ourselves."

We all nodded.

"Marcella, I will have you drop the halyard down so the rest of us can pull the sail in. Okay?"

She nodded, her face white with fear.

Jonas fired up the engine and adjusted the course so the wind blew the sail back onto the boat. The sail billowed and flapped, and the four of us positioned ourselves along the lifeline. Jonas made sure we were all secure in our harnesses and clipped onto the boat before he gave Marcella the signal to start lowering the sail.

Reaching as high as he could, Jonas grabbed the sail and tugged. Eivind pulled on the sheet until he could reach the sail and he gripped it and dragged it down too.

"Elayna, switch with me and keep the part on the deck from filling with wind again," Jonas said. Elayna crouched and tried to organize the mess of sail that piled up. Edges kept catching the wind and flapping.

Suddenly the sail stopped descending. Without the downward momentum, it filled with wind and started to blow out to sea.

It pulled our crew as we struggled against it, and Elayna slid along the deck of the boat until she slammed against the lifelines.

"Drop it down, Marcella, drop it down!" Jonas shouted.

The sail dropped again, faster this time, and we watched in horror as the top of the sail blew overboard and into the water.

"MARCELLA, PUT THE ENGINE IN NEUTRAL!" Eivind bellowed.

We dragged the sail beside us, but it, too, dragged us. We struggled with our grips on the sail, braced ourselves against whatever we could find, and it still wasn't enough. Next to me, Eivind's back strained, trying to not lose the sail.

I glimpsed down into the water as Eivind grunted with effort. The top half of the sail was overboard, and as we pulled, I could see the sail had scooped up water, weighing it down.

"We need to pull from the side!" I shouted.

"I can't let go!" Eivind gritted out.

I let go of my part and quickly slid around his body. I started pulling at the sail, trying to find the side of the spinnaker so I could release the water trapped in the billows. Finally I found the red tape lining the edge of the sail and pulled, dumping the water back into the ocean and releasing the weight.

Jonas, Elayna, and Eivind heaved again and the sail started to come up, soaked and salty. Hand over hand, we pulled it the rest of the way up and fell back onto the deck, piled on top of the thin material.

We were quiet, panting and stunned into silence.

"Jesus," Eivind whispered.

We slowly started to move, as if testing limbs and shaking them from sleep. Eivind pulled me close, tucking me into his body. His hands shook, exhausted from the strain.

"Are you okay?"

I nodded against his chest.

Footsteps came up behind me and I turned to find Marcella gripping the shroud in one hand, tears streaming down her face.

"Jonas, I'm so—" She broke off in a sob.

Jonas climbed to his feet and walked over, wrapping Marcella in his arms and cooing gently to her.

"The line . . . there was a twist. I couldn't . . . sorry . . ."

"Hey," Jonas said. "It is okay. We are all safe, and the boat is okay."

Eivind chuffed a laugh underneath my cheek. "I cannot believe the sail is back on deck. It is a miracle it did not catch on the keel or the propeller."

"That could happen?" I asked. "The sail floats though . . ."

He shook his head. "You saw how it filled with water. If we had been going too fast it would have been sucked under the boat. That would have been bad. We could have lost our engine."

Eivind's words weren't making me or Marcella feel much better. Jonas hushed him softly, rocking Marcella a little bit. "We are okay, the boat is okay," he kept repeating.

When Marcella calmed down, we started to move, gathering the sail to put it into the bag for now. Jonas didn't want to deal with it today and the sail needed to be checked over before we could deploy it again. It would be out of commission for the rest of the passage.

With the sail put away and nothing left for me to do to help, I climbed back downstairs and sank into bed, exhausted.

———————

WHEN I WOKE UP AGAIN, EIVIND WAS NOT IN BED WITH me. In fact, his side of the bed hadn't changed at all.

I dressed, wandered out, and found him in the cockpit.

"Hey, babe," I said. "Did you come to bed?"

"No, I let Jonas go down and rest. He needed it."

"That was nice of you." I ran my fingers over his cheek. He leaned into my touch. "Can I get you anything? Coffee?"

He smiled up at me. "Coffee would be nice."

I moved around downstairs, making us both coffee and dicing some fruit.

Back up in the cockpit, I snuggled against Eivind while we sipped our coffee and ate our fruit. Eivind liked pineapple the best, so I picked the chunks out and fed them to him.

"I like how you take care of your brother."

Eivind looked at me skeptically. "What do you mean? He is the older, responsible one. He has helped my mum take care of me since I was a child."

I shook my head. "Yeah, nah. You may be younger and more laid-back, but when Jonas is stressed, when he needs you, you're there for him." I fed him another chunk of pineapple. "You both strained and struggled with the sail today, but you let him relax more. You gave him time off."

"We did both work hard, but with Jonas, he has this big added responsibility. It is heavy." Eivind looked away from me, out at sea. "I do not think he thought it would be this hard." He chuckled darkly. "I am sure everyone says that. But also, we might be living this dream lifestyle, you know. People think, 'Oh, you sail and visit beautiful beaches—what stress can you have?' But it is not that."

Eivind trailed off, deep in thought. I finished my fruit and put the bowl beside me. We stayed quiet, the firm press of our bodies comforting each other.

"Sometimes," he confessed, "I do not think Jonas likes this very much. Maybe he would quit if it was just himself."

I pulled my head back a little to look up at Eivind. "You should talk to him about it."

The Hitchhiker in Panama

He blinked down at me and smiled. "Maybe I will."

Thirty-Three

EIK CHUGGED ALONG PEACEFULLY, THE ONLY sign of our previous trouble being that we didn't have the spinnaker out. Instead we had to sail what was called wing on wing, where the mainsail was on one side of the boat, the genoa on the other, and the wind came in from directly behind us. It was slower and less comfortable.

While *Eik* showed no signs of damage, the crew was not so lucky. Tensions were higher, and Eivind and I were crankier than normal.

Unfortunately, first thing in the morning Eivind had to get out on the deck and wash off presents from overnight visitors: birds had landed on the lifelines and shit on the deck.

After cleanup, Eivind sat on watch in the bright daytime, and we curled up together in the corner of the cockpit, reading. We hadn't seen a boat in weeks, so we just did regular checks on the horizon every fifteen minutes, and with the autopilot, *Eik* took care of herself.

Elayna popped up, asking if we wanted any coffee. We both declined, and she began pulling out supplies, muttering to herself. Cabinet doors slammed, and Eivind and I exchanged concerned looks.

"Eivind, have you seen the Nutella?"

He shifted to lean down and look through the companionway toward Elayna. "No, I have not."

He paused for a moment, listening. Marcella's loaves of bread, fresh from the oven only hours earlier, sat on the counter. When they'd first come out, the smell had been torture, and when the loaves were cool enough, we'd all had a slice or two. Now, though, I was thinking about a warm Nutella toastie.

"Oh crap, that sounds good."

Eivind threw me a smirk, but then a shriek came from the galley.

"WHAT ARE YOU DOING?" Marcella yelled.

Eivind and I scrambled down the companionway. Marcella stared in horror at the mayhem of the galley in the wake of Elayna's search party. Foodstuff was everywhere: she'd pulled everything out and stacked it all on the table, the counters, the floor. *Eik* swayed a bit more than usual on a wave and a few items toppled over and spilled onto the couch.

"Everything was organized, Elayna, by meals and categories. You can't just undo all of my work!"

"If it is so organized, then where is the Nutella?"

"I don't know. Have something else—don't tear my galley apart."

"It's not your galley."

"I do all the work in here."

Jonas stumbled out of his room. "What the hell is happening?"

"Someone ate all the Nutella," Elayna whined.

"I ate the Nutella." Jonas looked at her, bewildered. "It is for everyone."

Elayna groaned. "It is my favorite, and that was our last jar."

"You will have to have something else."

"You can have some Vegemite," I offered.

"Shut up!" Elayna snapped.

"Hey, watch it," Eivind said. "She is trying to help."

"How is that helpful?"

"It's an alternative!" Eivind threw up his hands. "The Nutella is gone, so move on."

"There is no alternative to Nutella."

Suddenly I didn't think we were talking about Nutella anymore.

"Okay, calm down, ja?" Jonas held his hands out imploringly. "This is only so bad because we are all feeling a little cabin fever right now. It is not a big deal."

Elayna crumpled, tears springing to her eyes. "Of course you do not think it is a big deal."

She stalked off to the cabin—the crew bunk she shared with Marcella—and slammed the door. Jonas shook his head, returning to his cabin and back to his nap. Eivind and I said nothing as he returned to his watch and I helped Marcella right the galley.

HOURS LATER MARCELLA WORKED ON DINNER, AND THE tension had not improved. Even though everything had been put away again, she was opening cabinets and huffing and muttering and slamming. Just watching her made me tense, like there would be an explosion.

I tried to help as best I could. Despite the boat's rocking, I was trusted with a sharp knife and was prepping some of our last vegetables. While I chopped, Marcella stirred, simmered, and baked circles around me.

"Take care of these." She handed me two cans that had held the marinara sauce now bubbling on the stove. I took them and, without thinking, pulled open the trash receptacle and threw them in.

The minute I closed the lid, I gasped. Marcella stared at me.

"Did you just do that?"

"Oh my gosh. I forgot I was supposed to wash them first. Marcella, I'm so sorry."

She tapped the spoon against the rim of the pot aggressively. "I am so careful in my galley. No food goes in the trash. Everything is washed and dried and condensed into as small of a shape as possible. I take care of these things, Lila!"

"I know, I am so sorry."

"You made a mistake, yes, but I will suffer. The trash will smell, and we only have so much space for trash," Marcella huffed.

"What is going on?" Eivind came down the stairs.

"I spilled tomato sauce in the trash bin."

Eivind leaned down and peeked into the trash. "I will help you clean it."

"Yeah, I guess so." I wrinkled my nose. Even clean trash was still trash.

"Lila can do it herself," Marcella snapped. "We have to be responsible for our own messes."

Eivind held up his hands. "Calm down, Marcella. We also are a team and help each other out."

"I just . . ." Marcella pinched the bridge of her nose. The room was quiet for a moment, save for the water rushing past *Eik*'s hull and the creaking of her lines. "Can you please finish dinner?"

"Of course," I murmured, and Marcella climbed the stairs into the cockpit.

———————

Elayna waited until the last minute to creep out of her room for dinner. I had been picking through every last piece of trash that had gotten tomato sauce on it, washing it and putting it in the sink drain. Eivind got dinner on the table. A few times I'd peeked outside to find Marcella looking small and a little lost, curled up in the corner of the cockpit and staring out to sea.

We called her down, and the five of us sat around the table. For a few minutes we were noisy with the clatter of tableware and dishes, asking for things and making yummy noises.

"Sleeping with other crew members is a bad idea. I was a little worried about Lila joining us on this trip, and I didn't say anything. I am sorry," Marcella said.

Eivind looked at me and cleared his throat. "Lila and I are fine, Marcella."

"You are fine, sure, but it still changes the dynamic, even if you are happy. It's not a good idea." She paused. "Do you remember when we met in Antigua? And I had been kicked off *Odyssey*?"

"Ja," Jonas said.

"It was because I slept with Seb. And my captain found out."

Jonas put his fork down. "Marcella . . . you did not tell us that."

"I was embarrassed."

Jonas touched her shoulder, and she waved his concern away.

"I knew it could happen," she went on, "and I did it anyway. So I had to leave. It was unprofessional of me, and while I am glad to be on board this boat, I miss the dynamic of professional crew."

We were silent for a moment.

"And maybe," she said with a slight smile, "I miss land a lot."

Neither Eivind nor I were sleeping. Eivind tossed and turned, kicking and stretching. I had an itch that would *not go away.*

"Eivind! Jesus!" I huffed as he flipped over again. "What is going on over there?"

"I was too busy cleaning bird shit off the boat to exercise this morning, and then it got hot, and I feel . . . just *uncomfortable.*"

"Yeah, well, I've got something going on with my bum. Seriously, it's so itchy!"

"Really?" Eivind switched on the light and sat up in bed. "Let me see."

I turned over, throwing a leg over his lap and burying my face in the mattress. Eivind's hand smoothed my skin, and he clucked his tongue.

"You have a rash here. Did you shower today?"

"Just before bed. It's so hot, there's no point in showering during the day. I'm just going to get sweaty again."

"Lila," he chided, "we are lucky enough to have a watermaker, and you can do a quick rinse twice a day, especially with the cockpit as wet as it has been lately. If you are sitting on damp cushions or shorts, you will get a rash."

I whimpered into the sheets. "The shower's just so small, and when the boat rolls a lot . . . I'm not seasick, but it's still uncomfortable."

"I know." He patted my butt. "Hold on, I have some cream." Eivind threw on shorts and grabbed his headlamp before disappearing into the hallway. He was back a few minutes later, and he sat on the bed and pulled me into his lap.

"This is not too bad. I have seen worse."

I wrinkled my nose. "Do I want to know how bad it gets?"

"Well, we had a friend who crossed the Atlantic without a watermaker, and he got becalmed for a few days. If you do not have fresh water, you rinse off in salt water more often, and when he arrived in the Caribbean, he had a rash all over his entire body."

"Ew."

"An even worse one . . . we watched a documentary at a film festival about these two guys who rowed across the Atlantic. They ended up having to, ah . . . drain the boils on each other's butts."

"Eivind! Gross!" I swatted at him, and he laughed.

"It did look painful."

"I bet. Well, no boils on my bum, right?"

"Hmm . . . I may have to do a big inspection," he teased, running his hands over me. "No boils. But you might want to think about doing your watches downstairs during the day now. You can check the horizon from the windows and use the downstairs electronics. And there is a fan we can blow onto the desk. You will not be wet from the waves, and you might sweat less."

"Okay. Thank you."

"You are welcome, darling." He kissed me quickly on the lips and rolled over onto his back.

I followed him, resting on my side, and swung a leg over Eivind's. "I know you missed your workout this morning, but you could do a different workout . . ."

Thirty-Four

I HAD A LAZY MORNING. EIVIND WAS UP ON WATCH, BUT, having nothing better to do, I stayed in bed and read.

My phone alarm went off at 11:45—it was time for my shift. I dressed and opened the door to the main salon where Marcella prepped lunch. Most of our meals nowadays were some variation of bread and canned meat. Yesterday had been tuna; today was pâté. As bland as eating out of cans seemed, Marcella always managed to pull out a treat to go with it: spicy mustard or capers. Add in the homemade bread, and lunches were shockingly amazing.

I made my plate from the smorgasbord platter on the table and climbed up to the cockpit. Eivind sat in the sun, one headphone in his ear, arms stretched out on either side, staring up at the sky.

When I sat next to him, he didn't move except for his head, watching me with a small smile on his face. I offered him a bite of my lunch and he growled, biting ferociously into the bread. I giggled.

His alarm went off at noon and he stood up and stretched. Leaning over, he pressed a kiss to my lips.

"Ready for your watch?"

I nodded, swallowing my last bite of food.

Setting the plate down on the cushion, I sat up and we both turned our attention to the electronics.

"Since we are so close now"—Eivind zoomed the chartplotter out so we could see our final destination—"we have the autopilot set to take us to this waypoint." Eivind pointed at a red X on the chart. "That means instead of the boat moving with the wind, we have to adjust the sails and the boat stays on course."

"Okay, so what do I need to watch for?"

"No numbers this time. You need to listen to the sails. If you hear the sails flapping or the boat starts to heel over too much, get Jonas."

"No numbers?" I frowned. "How will I know if the boat is heeling too much?"

He just kissed my forehead. "You will know."

I harrumphed. I didn't like the sound of subjective sailing.

Eivind chuckled and went downstairs.

I kept an eye on everything like I always did. Not long after I was left alone at the helm, the sails started to flap.

Poking my head down into the main salon, I called out, "Jonas, the sails are flapping."

"On my way."

A few moments later Jonas stood beside me at the helm.

"So, what do we need to do?" he asked.

"What? You are supposed to tell me that."

Jonas grinned. "You have read the sailing book—many times, I think. Tell me what you think we need to do and I will tell you if you are right."

"Okay, the sail is luffing, which means the wind has come too far forward. So . . . we have to tighten up the sails a little bit, right?"

"Ja."

"And the genoa is . . ." I put my hand on a winch with a line around it. "This one?"

He nodded. I grabbed the winch handle from its holder and fit it to the winch. I pushed the handle one way—nope, too hard—I pushed it the other way for the higher gear, then cranked with one hand, then two, breaking into a sweat.

"Is that enough?"

Jonas leaned out of the cockpit to look at the sail. "Not yet."

I took a deep breath and cranked a few more turns.

"That is good."

I wiped the sweat off my brow.

"What will you do next?"

Looking over my shoulder, I spotted the traveler. "The mainsail."

Unsnapping the handle, I moved it to the aft winch. I went to run the line around the barrel, and remembered that the handle gets in the way—I had to run the line around first without the handle on.

With the line secured around the winch, I started cranking again. Above me, the main sheet tightened, bringing the sail in closer to the centerline of the boat. This time I could see the sail better, and watched as the angle of the sail changed and it stopped luffing.

I glanced at Jonas. "Now?"

"Now. Great job, Lila!"

He offered me a high five and I laughed.

"I can't believe I could get all that by myself— mostly."

"You would have done it all by yourself. It is easier to see the genoa from here, but you would have gotten it."

I sat back down at the helm, smiling to myself. For the first time on this voyage, I felt like a sailor. Could I give all this up?

———————

Later that afternoon, I puttered around inside the cabin. The seas were unusually calm, so we'd opened some of the hatches that were less likely to get splashed by a wave. I ran around the cabin, shaking out our linens, clothes, even our towels, trying to freshen everything up.

Jonas, Elayna, and Eivind talked in the cockpit, their conversation coming in through the open hatch, but I wasn't paying attention until I heard my name.

"Lila must be looking forward to being on land?" That was Elayna. I paused and listened while folding a shirt that was slightly damp but still wearable.

"I think she is. I know she is not really a sailor, and it has been tough on her," Eivind responded.

My heart thudded in my chest. *Not really a sailor?* I knew so much more than when I'd started. Sure, I still didn't know how to read a tell-tail and I got confused by the compass, but I knew how to reef a sail, and I'd been on watch for over forty-eight hours by myself. How could he not think of me as a sailor?

"It will be nice when things go back to normal," Jonas said.

"What do you mean? Not at sea?" Eivind asked.

"Well, that too, but it will be better when it is just the four of us again. Lila has learned a lot, but it is harder to have to teach someone new. It is too hard when I have to teach someone how to sail, too."

"Marcella is right," Elayna said. "Crew dynamics are tough. Maybe we shouldn't have had her on in the first place."

"Well, she is going back to South America anyway," Eivind said. "She made it clear it was never long-term."

I bit my lip to stop myself from crying. Yes, the plan had always been for me to fly back once we reached land, but part of me had hoped that Eivind liked having me around and that maybe they'd invite me to stay again. Jonas and Eivind had made me feel so welcome in the beginning. To hear that maybe they regretted it?

Maybe everyone back home was right. Maybe I wasn't cut out for adventures.

EIVIND AND I HAD A QUIET NIGHT WATCH, BOTH OF US trapped in our own thoughts. I tried not to let myself spiral, but perhaps these past few weeks had been a waste.

And then I looked out at the night sky, spotting the band of the Milky Way overhead. The light mist of *Eik* plowing through the waves dusted my skin. Even if some people didn't consider me to be a true sailor, I had still crossed an ocean. I had sailed thousands of miles, and not many people could say that.

We had gone to bed knowing that when we woke up, we would likely see land. When Eivind's shift was over in the early hours of the morning, we were seventy miles from Fatu Hiva, the closest island in the chain of the Marquesas. While we couldn't legally enter the country there, we would stop for a day, visit the island reputed to be one of the most beautiful in the world, and then move on to Hiva Oa.

Fatu Hiva had minimal facilities, but Jonas and Eivind talked about it with such reverence. After crossing the Pacific—what would be most sailors' longest passage—Fatu Hiva provided a welcome sight.

When I woke up to voices above my head, I gently pushed Eivind's arm off me and dressed. He didn't stir, his face pressed into the pillow.

I kissed his shoulder and snuck out. I was too excited at the possibility of seeing land to stay down.

Giggles carried from the main salon and I found Jonas and Elayna inside. Jonas sat at the desk working on his laptop, and Elayna washed dishes in the galley.

"Papayas," said Jonas.

"Oohhh, *oui*, with some lime on them. I want a real baguette." Elayna closed her eyes and sniffed the air. "Fresh out of the oven."

"What about you, Lila?" Jonas asked. "What are you looking forward to?"

"A long walk."

Elayna sighed dreamily and Jonas grinned. "That one I can deliver today, I hope."

It gave me more energy just knowing we would be in port soon, stepping on land and getting out of this space that had once seemed so large to me.

Climbing out onto the deck, I looked ahead to *Eik*'s bow. Beyond it, on the horizon, Fatu Hiva towered. The island was steep, and cliffs dropped dramatically to the ocean. While it was still too far away for me to make out details, the island was a splotch of green—green!—in an eternal sea of blue.

Eventually the rest of the crew joined me and we watched the island approach. Eivind and I sat on the edge of the deck, hands gripping the lifelines and our legs dangling over the side. Occasionally the water tickled our toes when the boat rolled a bit deeper.

"What do you think?" Eivind asked.

"The island's beautiful." And it was. Now that we were closer, we could see the details: individual trees poking above the rest and shorebirds wheeling around the peaks.

"Would you do this again? Sail across an ocean?"

I wrinkled my nose. "It has been a very long trip. I would need a hell of a lot more books."

Eivind smiled out at the sea. "The next few weeks will be a lot better. We have small islands to visit, beautiful places, lots of snorkeling to do."

My stomach fluttered. In Panama, we had always said we'd part ways, even if we made it across the ocean together. But our relationship had grown and changed so much. Would he still want me to leave?

Jonas started up the engine, and that was our cue. We all worked together to bring the sails down. We motored into the Bay of Virgins. The steep walls surrounded us and the sea calmed.

Thirty-Five

WE PILED INTO THE DINGHY LIKE WIGGLING PUPPIES, eager to walk on land. We tied the dinghy up to a concrete wall, and one by one stepped onto shore.

I took a few shaky steps and almost face-planted into the grass. Elayna grabbed my arm and, with a gentle "oopla," guided me down.

"Whoa. Why does it feel like this? It's like I'm drunk and dizzy." I flopped down hard on the grass, but the world kept spinning.

"Your brain got used to being at sea. Give it a few minutes to recalibrate," Jonas said.

Elayna sat down next to me and lay on her back. She sighed. "Grass."

The rest of the crew lay down too, whether landsick or not. We all spent a few minutes lying back in the grass, staring up at the trees.

"It used to be the Bay of Penises," Eivind said next to me.

"Why did they change it?"

He shrugged. "Missionaries."

After a few minutes, I rolled over and experimentally sat up. Eivind watched me carefully. I made it in a few steps but managed to climb to my feet and dust myself off. "I think I'm okay."

"Great," Jonas said, and climbed to his feet.

We walked along the only road and stopped at a bulletin board with some postings on it. One was a map to a waterfall, which Eivind took a picture of with his phone.

Continuing along, we walked past small houses with lush gardens. We were in the jungle, where everything was thick and green. Fruit grew everywhere—massive breadfruit and mango trees, papayas, coconuts. Kids played in the streets, and dark-haired Polynesian women swept their gravel driveways.

Most people called out to us: "Bonjour!"

We all called back, but Elayna would strike up a conversation in French. Often, she pointed at plants and asked what was growing. At one of the houses, some older boys ran around, and after a conversation with the woman of the house, Elayna consulted with Marcella.

Marcella had packed a backpack with bottles of water and snacks for us, but also a few smaller items. "For trading," she had said.

Elayna pulled out some small baggies of rice and sugar. She conversed with the woman and pointed to the boys. The two women agreed and Elayna waved goodbye, leaving the sugar and rice behind.

"This woman will have fresh coconuts for us to drink when we walk back. Her son will climb up the tree for us."

Yum, I thought.

We continued on the road. Chickens pecked around the underbrush, and deeper in the woods wild pigs occasionally grunted.

A man ran past us—pale and blond. Eivind and Jonas shared a look.

"Gendarme?" Eivind said quietly.

"Maybe."

"What's a gendarme?" I asked.

"The local French police. We could get in trouble for being on this island without clearing into the country first. Everyone does it, but occasionally they do patrol and fine you."

A few minutes later another European passed us, a woman.

"Gendarmette?" Eivind whispered, and I giggled.

At the side of the road, we found our first cairn, a stack of rocks marking a path for travelers. We veered off the roads and into the jungle, following the well-worn path. Huge hibiscus flowers polka-dotted the trail beneath our feet.

We followed cairn after cairn, climbing higher and higher. The whole time, we couldn't help pointing things out to one another; we were all so wide-eyed with wonder, hardly anything went unnoticed.

The thunder of the waterfall crescendoed just before we turned the corner and spotted it. It poured down off a sheer cliff, easily a hundred meters high. At the base was a small pool with clear, cold water, deep enough for us to swim.

We stripped down to our underwear and splashed around in the pool. It was about ten meters wide by fifteen meters long, and by swimming across the length we could duck under the falls and look out from behind the curtain of water. Everything was slick with moss or algae.

When we tired—which was quick—we sat on rocks, drying ourselves in the warm air.

We walked back lazily, finding the house with the coconuts. A small pile of husked coconuts sat on the lawn. The boys hacked at the shells with machetes, cutting a square out of the top of the coconut and prying it off.

When we each had a coconut, I wondered how to gracefully drink it. Eivind put his mouth on the opening and tried to drink quickly, spilling it all over himself in the process. The boys giggled at him, and the lady scolded them in French.

The boys then went to a nearby papaya plant and pulled off leaves from the trunk of the tree. Snapping the leaf from the stalk, they presented us with the hollow petiole.

Elayna exchanged a few words. "Ah! Straws!" She put the stem in her coconut and sipped the water up through the straw. "Voilà!"

We followed her example and the coconut water hit my tongue, slightly tangy and refreshing. Eivind was the first one to chug his down.

With the machete, one of the boys took a big swing and cracked the coconut in half. He showed Eivind how to use the top square as a spoon to scoop out the flesh. He repeated his machete-swinging skills for all of us, and we ate the soft jelly from the inside of the coconut.

Before we could leave, the woman went into her house and returned with a small plastic bag full of mangoes. She gave Elayna the bag, and we all thanked her in our limited French: "Merci!" Elayna kissed her cheeks and we set out for the dock.

Unfortunately, we could not rest any further. Jonas wanted to get under sail again after dinner, which would allow us to arrive at Hiva Oa early in the morning, where we would clear in.

OVER DINNER, MARCELLA PUT HER FORK DOWN.

"I have been thinking a lot about the upcoming time in French Polynesia. I have enjoyed being with each of you, but I think it is time for me to move on and leave the boat."

Everyone froze. Jonas and Eivind exchanged glances.

"Is this because of the spinnaker situation?" Jonas asked.

"In part." Marcella inhaled a shaky breath. "The sailing, with watches and sail changes, is too much for me. I don't know how you do it, Jonas; it's too much pressure." Her eyes filled with tears, and Elayna pulled Marcella into her side for a hug.

Jonas sighed and squeezed her hand. "I understand. When do you want to leave? In Hiva Oa?"

Marcella composed herself. "When do you think *Eik* will arrive in Tahiti?"

Jonas ran his fingers through his hair. He hadn't had a hair cut in a long time and it was shaggy. "Three or four weeks, I think? I am sorry, Marcella, I cannot guarantee—"

Marcella interrupted him. "I know how it goes. That is fine. I will start to look for a new position, or maybe ask around some boats near here. I will find something."

Eivind cleared his throat, poking his food around with his fork. "It's not usually this hard. We do not—" He swallowed. "We do not have a big sail like that again. This will be better." His voiced cracked and he glanced up, but not at Marcella. At me.

The rest of dinner was quiet, with Eivind's palm a heavy weight on my thigh. I looked up several times to find him watching his brother, concern etched deep into his face. Sometimes our eyes met; he watched me. We cleaned up, keeping our voices low, and got the boat underway again just before sunset.

For the first time since we'd departed Panama, we didn't watch the sunset together, instead retreating to our own corners.

I stripped down and crawled into bed, Eivind close behind me. He ran his palm, his nose, his lips up my curves. We lay face-to-face as he slipped into me, deep wet kisses and tangled legs.

The moment I felt a tremor deep in my belly, the first tear slipped down my cheek. Eivind kissed it away. Rolling me onto my back, he kissed each tear, murmuring to me in Norwegian words I was sure would break my heart.

Marcella's confession had opened the floodgates, allowing me to realize the deep sense of relief that the journey was nearly over. I sobbed and clung to Eivind, and we held each other till we fell asleep, too worn down to think of anything else.

Thirty-Six

I HADN'T JOINED EIVIND FOR HIS WATCH THE NIGHT before. Physically and emotionally exhausted, I'd slept straight through it.

When I woke up, the brothers were dropping anchor at Hiva Oa.

Once settled, we piled into the dinghy and went to shore. Our yacht agent met us at the wharf and drove us over to the town in the back of her pickup truck.

"How much does an agent cost?"

Jonas shook his head. "A few hundred euros. But the agent will get us paperwork for duty-free fuel and exempt us from having to post a thousand-euro bond per person."

We slipped into the office with gendarmes and filled out paperwork, had our passports stamped, and practiced our polite French, though everyone spoke English.

Our agent dropped us off at the top of the hill overlooking the anchorage. There was a small shipping container and some picnic tables set up. During the day, the agent would open the container and turn on the Wi-Fi for the cruisers to use. We settled at the tables and soon the air filled with a chorus of dings as notifications began flooding in.

I quickly scanned my emails, looking for anything important. My phone pinged with all kinds of social media notices, which I ignored. I fired off a few emails and pulled up a flight website to check for rates and schedules.

Flights were expensive, but I knew that would happen. I sat staring at the purchase button for a while, playing the last few weeks over and over in my mind. So many emotions flooded through me as I finally booked my flight—sadness to be leaving *Eik* and the crew behind, the heartbreak when I thought of Eivind. I tried to focus on the relief. I could stretch my legs, walk every day, meet new people, get back on track with my plans.

I would fly out the next day to Tahiti, and then two nights later fly to Lima.

I STARTED PACKING UP MY STUFF. EIVIND WAS OUT ON deck with Jonas, doing some project, so I had the cabin to myself. In the small space, our stuff had comingled, and separating my things from Eivind's was making me angry. Here was Eivind's jade-green shirt that brought out his eyes, the top that Eivind had practically ripped off me during an afternoon "nap," the sweater he'd lent me when I was cold on night watch.

When Eivind finally came in, I had lined one of my backpacks with a bin liner and tried to shove my dirty clothes in. The backpack was mostly zipped, but I shoved a finger in and wriggled, trying to make room for one last pair of undies.

He looked around at the mayhem for a few moments while I tried to ignore him. Sweeping some of his clothes aside, he sat down on the edge of the bed next to me.

"You do not have to go, you know."

I let his words hang for a moment. "Well, it seems like I'm not a good enough sailor to be here." I hated the way my voice came out, petty and hurt.

"What? Wait, Lila. No, that is not true."

"It is true. I'm not a sailor, and I've just been a liability and an added stress. Look, Eivind, this was the deal, right? I stay to sail across the Pacific, I get my adventure in, and I move on. Mission accomplished."

"We did not really mean it. The last few days have been stressful, and everyone is tired."

"What, you think Jonas didn't mean it when he said he wanted things back to normal?"

Eivind winced. "He is just—"

"Don't say he's stressed, Eivind!" I threw up my hands. "This is his boat, he's the captain. We're all tired. I'm tired of being here." I went back to work trying to close the zipper of my backpack.

"It was not just stress. He was just agreeing with Elayna. Things have been hard enough with her as it is."

"I just don't understand that. I really like you, Eivind, and I think you really like me. I don't understand their relationship, but they aren't even together. So why try to make Elayna feel good while throwing me under the bus? Why sacrifice our relationship?"

"I do not know," Eivind ground out, frustration edging his words. He ran a hand over his head and stood up to pace. I watched him for a moment, arms crossed, but he was at a loss for words.

"I think," I said, "that you are trying so damn hard to sacrifice yourself for any tiny chance to make your brother happy. But what about you, Eivind? You put your whole life on hold to help your brother sail across oceans. What makes you happy?"

"I did not put anything on hold. I had no real job, a shitty apartment, it was no sacrifice."

"Ah, so you needed a worthy sacrifice."

Eivind stopped pacing and looked at me.

"And that's me."

His eyes widened, and he rushed toward me. "That is not true!"

I held a hand up, holding him back. "If that's not true, then come with me. We can go backpack together. Jonas has Elayna, he can get more crew members; he can sail with them to New Zealand. It would give us a real chance."

"We could have a real chance here on *Eik*." Eivind ran a hand up my arm and, without intending to, I leaned into it. Eivind took the opportunity, and we swayed into each other.

Eivind's arms wrapped around me, solid and warm. But I could feel the strain, the weight of sadness pressing down on him. I gripped him hard, pressing my face into his chest.

He inhaled, deep and shaky. "I want you here with me." His voice broke, and we held each other tight.

When I finally pulled back, we were both sniffling.

"Take me to shore?" I asked quietly.

He nodded.

Thirty-Seven

THE CREW SAID GOODBYE TO ME AT THE DOCK, AND WE ALL exchanged contact information. The agent had arranged a car to take me to a local hostel. Jonas and Elayna pulled me aside before Eivind said goodbye.

"Eivind told me you heard our conversation," Jonas said. "We just wanted to say we are so sorry for suggesting you were not good enough. You were really great."

I smiled weakly. "For someone who doesn't know how to sail, right?"

Elayna grimaced and looked down.

Jonas leaned in. "Do not break up with him because I said something I should not have said. I mean it, Lila. You should stay."

I looked away, and after a beat, Eivind moved in to hug me goodbye. We embraced, and I inhaled deeply, taking in those scents of lemon and sunshine, hoping to imprint them on my memory. Eivind gripped the back of my head before I could pull away, planting kisses on my hair, my forehead, and down my face. He allowed himself one press to my lips then took a step back. I pulled away quickly and climbed into the car before I could change my mind.

AT MY HOSTEL, I IMMEDIATELY CRAWLED ONTO MY BUNK bed in the dorms. The bed was rickety and narrow, even compared to *Eik*'s crew bunks, where I'd only spent one night. It was too early to expect anyone to allow me a moment's quiet: the doors constantly opened, conversations carried on around me, and something reeked horribly from the far corner of the room. Perhaps I'd just gotten used to the fresh air and sea breeze.

After a few hours of that, bone-weary but unable to ignore the stimulation around me, I got up and trudged into the common area. I turned my phone on and connected to the free Wi-Fi.

A chorus of chirps demanded my attention as a series of messages from my mother arrived.

Did you leave the boat okay?

313

Was your flight today?

Are you in Tahiti?

Lila?

Lila, I just emailed with Jonas. He said you got to the hostel okay. Where are you?

And one from Marcella.

Hi. We miss you already. Have a good flight.

I tapped over to my mum's messages and her increasing panic. I sighed and tapped the phone icon.

She answered on the first ring. "Please tell me you are off that godforsaken boat."

I burst into tears.

My mum, God bless her, cooed into the phone while I scrambled to collect myself again.

"Your father's here. I'm putting you on speakerphone." The phone emitted some muffled noises while Mum figured out the app. She said to my father, "Lila's upset."

Dad's voice came on the line. "I told that young man I'd cut his balls off."

I laughed despite myself.

"You sound very upset, sweet pea. What's going on?"

I told my parents everything in a huge flood of words. I told them, as best I could, the struggles and hardships of what twenty-six days at sea had been like.

Now that I was off the boat, it seemed different. Flattened. Like I'd had huge emotional swings that rocketed around *Eik* with no way to get out. Now, without the ground swaying beneath me or the wind in my face, all of my feelings rushed out.

It was cathartic.

"I thought the sail was boring?" Mum said.

"It was. Kind of. There's an old saying Jonas told me, that sailing is boredom with flashes of sheer terror." I winced, expecting Mum to zero in on the terror like a hawk. Instead she said something that surprised me.

"Tell me about the good parts."

So I sat back in the chair and told my parents about the endless blue of the ocean, stargazing with Eivind, eating freshly caught fish. I talked about helping to hoist the sails, the feel of the winch handle in my palm and the burn of my muscles as I cranked the sail in.

My parents listened quietly. When I finished, Dad spoke up.

"What about Eivind?"

I told them about our fight, my cheeks burning with embarrassment when I admitted to my parents that their daughter had not, in fact, become a sailor.

"Well, I didn't expect you to be! It was only a month at sea, really," Mum said.

"Mum!"

"What? It's true."

"Well, it still hurts my feelings."

"Yes, well, it was rather rude of them to say that. They owe you an apology. I might have to write Jonas a stern letter."

"They did apologize, and Jonas said I am welcome to stay on the boat. Save your letter-writing for someone else who deserves your wrath."

"Disappointing." She tsk-tsked. "So then, the real heart of the matter, do you want to be back on the boat?"

"It's just . . . I thought getting off the boat would be easier. Life would be easier. But . . ." I looked around the hostel at all these strangers, smoking weed, drinking beer, having loud conversations in nearly a dozen languages. Suddenly it seemed irritating and dull. How could it compete with the wide-open ocean? I closed my eyes and thought of Eivind's joyful warmth, Jonas's quiet reserve, the colors of the sea, and the gloss and shine of *Eik*.

"You feel conflicted?" Dad asked.

I opened my eyes. "Yeah. I do."

In the silence, my mum sighed, resigned. "She's in love."

I didn't argue. I'd never felt this way about someone before, so perhaps it was love.

"Well, *Eik* has plans, and Eivind is part of that."

"Why can't you stay on the boat?"

My mouth dropped open; I was shocked that my mum would even consider that option.

"I have plans," I said stubbornly. "Backpacking in South America."

"Yes, I know about those plans. I'm pretty sure you picked them just to piss me off. Sailing away with Eivind would accomplish the same goal."

I smiled. "It wasn't *all* about pissing you off, Mum." I picked at the corner of the table in front of me. "I did ask Eivind to come with me."

A heavy silence fell. "He said no?"

I sighed. "It was more important for him to stay with his brother than to be with me."

"Ah," Mum said. "'Never make someone a priority when all you are to them is an option.'"

"Something like that. It made me really angry at first, but the more I think about it, the more I can understand it. Eivind made his commitment to Jonas, and he doesn't want to back out and let his brother down."

"I think that's pretty admirable."

I groaned. "And I don't want him to give that up."

"It sounds like you might have just needed a break from the boat and the stress. There's nothing wrong with a time-out."

"It might be too late." I swallowed, regret thickening in my throat.

"Oh, sweetie. It's never too late."

Thirty-Eight

I CLIMBED DOWN THE STAIRS OF THE HOSTEL AND STARTED for the breakfast buffet. I needed some serious coffee. I'd slept fitfully the night before, tossing and turning, thinking about my conversation with Mum and the decisions I had to make. I wasn't sure if I missed the gentle rocking of the ocean or the warmth of Eivind's body pressed against me or both.

I pressed a mug under the dispenser and waited on the slow trickle of coffee. Someone walked up behind me to wait their turn.

"Morning," I muttered.

"God morgen" came a careful voice.

I spun so quickly, the coffee flew out of my mug, and Eivind barely managed to dodge it.

"Shite." I grabbed a handful of napkins to throw on the floor. Eivind helped, pressing the bottom of his shoes onto the napkins and rubbing them around.

"What are you doing here?" I exclaimed. And then I caught sight of his backpack on the ground beside him. I gripped his forearm. "Eivind, what are you doing here?" I repeated.

"I want to come with you." He shifted his feet, nervousness tightening his features.

"To South America?" I said slowly.

"Yes, but also, to Australia. And wherever else you want to go. I'll get a better job. A career, one that uses my degree, and we can live in Australia and buy a house."

I laughed in relief. "Eivind, hang on. We don't have to plan out everything right now."

He cracked a smile. "You want to make a spreadsheet later?"

"Very funny." I poked his side and then slid my arms around his waist. Eivind exhaled deeply and relaxed against me. "I am so glad you want to be with me." I squeezed him extra hard. "Thank you."

He pulled back and looked me in the eye, cupping my cheek and stroking it with his thumb. A tear rolled down, and he kissed it away. "I think it is a little crazy how much I love you after such a short time."

"I love you too. And I feel the same way. We've been through so much together already."

"Yes," he said. "We have only known each other for six weeks. But if we were dating in regular lives, that would have been, what? Ten or twelve dates?"

I tapped his nose with my finger. "Instead I've been stuck with you for a month. All day, every day."

Eivind hugged me tightly again. We stood there for a moment, the bustle of the hostel around us.

We finally pulled apart.

"I have not booked the flight yet. I am not sure if I can get the same one as you, but maybe I can use the internet here and try to book it?"

"Actually," I said, "I don't think I want to leave."

Eivind looked down at me quizzically.

"I accept Jonas's and Elayna's apologies. And I admit, I may have been a little overly sensitive and let my feelings get hurt."

"Ah, Lila. You *are* a good sailor."

"How about 'I show a lot of promise'?"

Eivind grinned at me. "Okay, that is fair."

"You know what makes a good sailor, Eivind?"

He tucked a strand of hair behind my ear. "No, what makes a good sailor, Lila?"

"Lots of practice. Why don't we go help Jonas sail to New Zealand?"

Eivind pulled back, shocked. "You would do this?"

"If I'm your priority, then you are mine. And I know how much it means to you to help your brother. Just promise me that if it gets to be too much, we find a solution together, okay?"

Eivind responded by pulling me close and crushing his lips against mine. I let him in, and he swept me up and squeezed me tight.

When we finally gasped for air, he managed to say, "I did not think I could love you more."

He moved to kiss me again and I stopped him. "Wait. We don't have to sail twenty-six days at sea again, do we?"

Eivind laughed. "No longer than a week in one go."

"Oh, thank God."

He kissed me again.

"And one more thing," I said.

Eivind raised an eyebrow.

"My parents are very supportive of me staying with you. So . . . when we get to New Zealand, we have to fly home to Australia for the holidays this year."

He groaned and loosened his grip on me. "I have to meet your dad."

"He's not scary!"

"He loves you, and I am the man sleeping with his daughter. Of course he is scary!"

I grinned and pressed my cheek into Eivind's chest. "I can't believe this is going to be my life now. Months ago I was so nervous to leave home. Now I'm going to sail around the South Pacific with the man I love."

He laughed, but then pulled back to look at me. "Are you sure this is the adventure you want?"

"Eivind," I said, wrapping my arms around his neck and pulling his lips down to mine, "you *are* my adventure."

Epilogue

A Few Weeks Later

EIK GLIDED ALONG THE STILL WATERS OF KAUEHI'S lagoon. The past few weeks had been a paradise of island hopping, from the beautiful, rugged islands of the Marquesas to the postcard-perfect atolls of the Tuamotus. Unlike the Marquesas, the Tuamotus were low, flat islands with sandy beaches, idyllic palm trees, and crystal-clear water. Less jungle exploration, more sandy beaches for bonfires and picnics.

Jonas was at the helm, lazily steering us along toward our destination—a beautiful and remote anchorage that we had hoped to have all to ourselves. Sailing boats were few and far between in these islands.

"Someone is already anchored there," Jonas said, disappointed.

I looked up from my book and scanned the horizon, finding the mast of a sailboat just off the beach.

"Bummer," I teased. "Company in paradise."

I settled back down, my feet in Eivind's lap. He squeezed my ankle and winked at me.

A few minutes later Jonas sat straight up in his seat. "Binoculars! Binoculars!" He frantically searched around the cockpit, upturning pillows. Eivind and I jolted into action, helping Jonas search the cockpit.

"Where are they?" Jonas muttered, and fired off what sounded like a Norwegian expletive.

My gaze landed on the binoculars sitting atop the helm station. "Jonas!" I said, exasperated. "Right here."

He grabbed them from me, holding them to his face and aiming at the sailboat in the anchorage.

"What is it?" Eivind asked his brother, climbing out of the cockpit and shading his eyes to take a closer look.

Eivind was too far away to hear the whispered words that came from Jonas. "It is *Welina*."

"Who's *Welina*?"

"*Welina*?" Eivind repeated. "I do not know this boat."

Jonas didn't answer but kept watching through the binoculars.

"Jonas," Eivind said firmly, "who is *Welina*?"

Finally Jonas pulled his eyes away and checked our course. "You watched their videos with me, remember? It is Mia and . . . Liam was her husband, but I heard things . . ." His voice trailed off.

Eivind contemplated the boat for a moment but then shook it off. Looking at me, he shrugged and headed up to the bow to prepare the anchor.

———————

AN HOUR LATER AND JONAS HAD BARELY TAKEN HIS EYES off the boat next to us. "Okay, explain to me what's going on with this boat."

Jonas stood in the main salon, staring out the window. "There is a sailing channel on YouTube called 'Welina Sailing.' I watched many of their videos. They are very popular, and I learned so much."

"You should go say hi. Right?" Eivind said.

Jonas turned away from the window and rubbed the back of his neck. "I do not know. It was a couple, but I read that they divorced. Maybe they sold the boat."

"Wait, is this the one with the long red hair and dimples?" Eivind asked.

Jonas paced the length of the salon and then returned to the window.

"Yes, I remember now. Mia. We watched some of those videos together, the day you asked me to come sailing with you."

"Yes" was all Jonas said.

Eivind and I exchanged bemused looks.

"It would be rude not to go over and say hi," I said. "After all, we are the only boats in the anchorage. You are just being polite." I winked at Eivind.

"Yes, okay." He started for the companionway before quickly turning around. "I should bring something." He opened the fridge and stuck his head in, pulling things out left and right.

"Hey, wait, stop!" Marcella got up and swatted Jonas away from the fridge. "It's organized. What do you want?"

"What would be a good gift to bring her? Wine? Or maybe one of the chocolate bars?"

"Who are you bringing a gift to?"

I turned around to find Elayna in the doorway, watching Jonas carefully.

When Jonas didn't answer, I did. "The neighbors."

"Why don't you take one of those tuna fillets over?" Marcella suggested. "Every sailor likes fresh fish."

"Ja, okay."

Five minutes later Eivind and I stood on the deck of *Eik* as Jonas paddled his way over to *Welina*. Eivind wrapped his arms around me.

"I think my brother has a crush," he said quietly.

The End

Thank you for reading.

Subscribers to my newsletter get special content:

-a bonus epilogue about the very special moment in Fakarava between Lila and Eivind

-photos and stories from my own trip through the Panama Canal and the Pacific Ocean

Sign up for my emails at lizalden.com.

Have you read the prequel short story,
The Night in Lover's Bay?

See how Marcella met the crew of Eik and started on her adventure. It's available to subscribers of my newsletter for free. Sign up and get your copy at lizalden.com.

Reviews are critical to all authors.
You can leave a review for *The Hitchhiker in Panama* at all retailers
Amazon | Kobo | Apple Books
Barnes & Noble | Google Books
and
Goodreads | BookBub

Also by Liz Alden:

Acknowledgements

So much went into my debut novel that you hold in your hands. Thank you to fellow writers Laurie, Lidia, and Trish, who read a very early (and very different) copy of this book. To sailors Behan, Viki, and Lloyd, thank you for your fact-checking and feedback.

I somehow threw together a great editing team on the first go round: Tiffany, who put many hours into this manuscript and made me rewrite a ton of it; Kaitlin, who polished this book like crazy; and David, another good polish, another sailor's feedback, and bonus tidbits from his own trip.

Elizabeth is the mastermind behind the cover I can't stop staring at.

A big thank you to my husband, who encouraged me so much from day one, and my parents, all five of them, who supported this book in one way or another.

About Liz Alden

Liz Alden is a digital nomad. Most of the time she's on her sailboat, but sometimes she's in Texas. She knows exactly how big the world is—having sailed around it—and exactly how small it is, having bumped into friends worldwide.

She's been a dishwasher, an engineer, a CEO, and occasionally gets paid to write or sail.

This is her debut novel.

For 100-word flash fiction stories, book reviews, and teasers for the *Love and Wanderlust* series, follow Liz.

lizalden.com

Made in the USA
Monee, IL
14 September 2021

78067002R00204